David S.E. Earl of Buchan

Essays on the Lives and Writings of Fletcher of Saltoun and the Poet Thomson

Biographical, critical, and political. With some pieces of Thomson's never before published

David S.E. Earl of Buchan

Essays on the Lives and Writings of Fletcher of Saltoun and the Poet Thomson
Biographical, critical, and political. With some pieces of Thomson's never before published

ISBN/EAN: 9783337012274

Printed in Europe, USA, Canada, Australia, Japan

Cover: Foto ©Raphael Reischuk / pixelio.de

More available books at **www.hansebooks.com**

ESSAYS

ON THE

LIVES AND WRITINGS

OF

FLETCHER OF SALTOUN

AND THE

POET THOMSON:

BIOGRAPHICAL, CRITICAL, AND POLITICAL.

With some Pieces of THOMSON's never before published.

———

BY *D. S. EARL OF BUCHAN.*

═══════

LONDON:

PRINTED FOR J. DEBRETT,
OPPOSITE BURLINGTON-HOUSE, PICCADILLY.

MDCCXCII.

CONTENTS.

Thomson's

CONTENTS.

An

A Hu-

viii   C O N T E N T S.

N. B. THE Four laft Articles were received by the Printer after all the others had gone to Prefs: otherwife the Earl of Buchan's Eulogy on Thomfon, according to a natural Arrangement, would have been introduced in the Conclufion of this Volume.

INTRODUCTION.

ALTHOUGH I am fensible that the very found and fight of the word LIBERTY has become difagreeable, if not terrible, to the fafhionable world in Britain; yet it is neceffary that I fhould introduce the Memoirs of Fletcher and Thomfon with reflections on the principles, manners, and temper, of the times and countries in which

B

they

they lived, and of thofe that preceded their appearance. It is my purpofe to treat this fub-ject very briefly.

It naturally divides itfelf into three parts; the Gothic, Puri-tanical, and Philofophical ages: under which three heads, with-out once mentioning the formi-dable and profcribed vocable, I fhall endeavour to make it clear and convincing to the meaneft and moft obdurate capacity, that political energy and fentiment were never wholly fuppreffed in my native country.

1ft. Political energy and fentiment eminently appeared in the Gothic, by which I literally denominate that age which was coeval with the formation of military governments on a feudal bafis, by the nations or people that over-ran Europe in ages far beyond the æra of genuine hiftory, formed the ftates of Greece and Italy, and afterwards in a more barbarous ftate overfpred and overpowered the Roman empire, which had fprung from the fame original.

But the fyftem of Gothic go-

vernment

vernment was permanent, and we have it accurately delineated by the mafterly hand of Tacitus, in his Treatife on the Situation, Cuftoms, and People of Germany.

In this æra, which is of immenfe duration, I obferve political energy and fentiment exemplified every where in the equal rights of the holders of the foil.

In countries and ages where lands were cultivated by flaves taken in war, or brought into bondage by conqueft, there could be no other citizens.

Trade and manufactures were not.

In such a posture of society sciences and arts could not exist.

The proprietors of the soil could not protect themselves without government; and government requires a prince either single or complex, elective or hereditary.

Governments were therefore formed variously, as contingency or necessity occasioned or required.---Scotland, the country to which my subject directs me,

was

was planted and governed in this manner from the beginning.

The miferable natives who preceded the Goths or Scythians, were treated like the natives of North and South America by the Europeans; and, after fkulking and fcalping for ages in their faftneffes, muft have at laft yielded to neceffity or reafon in their obedience to the laws of the ftrongeft.

In England, after the dereliction of the Roman provinces by the legions, the enervated flaves of imperial Rome became

an

an eafy prey to every hardy invader. *Veni, vidi, vici,* is a boaft no way honourable or peculiar to Cæfar.

The Saxons and Danes, to go no farther, exemplified the motto with a vengeance; and I fhall allow the baftard of Normandy to have been a King William, and to have come over to fave the miferable Englifh from Dane-gelt, flavery, and arbitrary power.

Great and big books have been written to fhew that Englifh law and liberty are as old

 as

as the country. I diflike big books, and leave Lord Lyttelton in poffeffion of the field.

If conftitutions of government could be juftly held to admit of no radical amendments, according to the political gofpel of Edmund, then the Gothic conftitution was as perfect as poffible.

But the rapid improvement of fociety foon rendered it odious, unjuft, and ridiculous.

To overthrow it, however, there was no people; for the king and the flaves were, in

fact,

fact, the only people, and the nobility was the prince.

The king, therefore, with the flaves, *aſſumed* the ſtation of the people, and cruſhed more or leſs in different ages and countries *the prince,* combined and compoſed of the great proprietors of the ſoil.

This was accompliſhed by exciting and quelling impotent rebellions, by leaguing with the clergy, eſtabliſhing free towns and corporations, and by encouraging trade and navigation.

James I. King of Scots,

was

was far advanced in this plan
when he was affaffinated by the
Earl of Athol.   He had gone fo
far to form a popular government by encouraging the leffer
barons and the boroughs of
Scotland, and by the attainder
of the great earls, that he ufed
to joke with his Queen (the
great grand-daughter of Edward
III.) faying, " My dear, I hope
the day is not far diftant when
I may have the pleafure of
finding you in bed with all the
nobility of Scotland!" a brave
project for a patriot prince, and
worthy

worthy of a more fortunate iſſue!

A rich and powerful nobility (alias an oligarchy) muſt ſoon deſtroy the liberties of any people among whom they are ſuffered to domineer.

It is neceſſary to explain what the King of Scots meant by *all the nobility of Scotland.*

They were the Earls and Lords of Regality.

Scotland never knew ſuch a monſtrous order of men as Lords of Parliament.

The Earls had no right to ſit

in

in the Parliament but by their lands; but being chief magistrates and judges in their counties, with regal powers, these, with their territorial advantages springing from the feudal system, rendered them truly formidable both to the king and to the commonwealth.

James saw the advantages reaped in England by the crown, in consequence of the formation of a peers house of parliament, and the power of calling up great commoners by writ of summons to that house of parliament, and

wished

wiſhed to adopt ſo crafty an example.

On the trial of Murdoch, Duke of Albany, he eſtabliſhed a precedent for what were called Barons of Baron-rent, to be called Lords and Nobles, and to ſit with precedence in the parliament by royal charter of lands, erecting eſtates into earldoms or baronies, uncon‑nected with the ancient earl‑doms or county palatines of the kingdom; and, then, by the election of certain members of parliament, for preparing the

laws

laws or acts, who were called the Lords of the Articles, chofen from the earls, barons of baron-rent, and the great officers of the ftate, he contrived to quafh or prevent motions that were adverfe to the intereft of the crown *.

I blufh to repeat the A B C of the political hiftory of Britain; but as I have not met with a fhort effence of it in any of our modern novels, I hope I may be excufed, at leaft, by ladies and gentlemen who feldom turn over unwieldy vo-

* See Burnet's Hiftory of his Own Times.

lumes.

lumes. Thus the creation of a tiers etat, or, of the weight of the people in the political balance, as is well obferved in Captain Newte's admirable Tour in Scotland, was not the work of patriots, but of kings. In Sir William Wallace, the *Tell* of Scotland, we have a precious unique in the Gothic age of Scottifh political energy and fentiment; and had Scotland belonged by hereditary claims to England or France, he would probably have engaged his countrymen to have formed a republic like the Swifs.

He

He was envied and hated by the earls and great barons of Scotland; and by *their* treachery he fell a martyr to the independency and liberties of his country. It is in vain to search for the moral and rational principles of government in the military Gothic age: in those wretched times men had no civic union, no proper interchange of political sentiment. Fixed, or rather chained as they were to the soil of their masters, the people were without collision of sentiment; had no organized societies for

the

the contemplation of common interefts; no high roads, no pofts, no printing-preffes! What is man in fuch a fituation, but the machine of regal or princely ambition and luxury!

II. I come now to confider the puritanical age of political energy and fentiment. Nothing could have been more fortunate for mankind, than the deftruction of the degraded Greek empire by the Turks, fo foon after the diffemination of the doctrines of Wickliffe, and the reformers of the church of Rome.

It

It gave Europe philofophers, and teachers, and men of learn-ing, Greek, and fenfe, and fpirit.

Human genius and fentiment are always moft agreeably ex-cited by the contemplation of misfortunes. We naturally attach ourfelves to the fide of the lofer of a conteft. The ftruggles for liberty in Greece and Italy, re-corded fo eloquently by the Greek and Roman claffics, im-bued the minds of youth, and excited the feelings of the aged with the ardour of political fen-timent. The people then began

to

to know truly what it is to be a member of a free commonwealth, to be a citizen: delightful name! beſt of inheritances, beſt of rights, not to be ſurrendered, but with the life that accompanies it! With theſe ſublime and heart-engaging affections, the ſtudy of the Scriptures of Moſes and the Evangeliſts in the living languages of Europe, and the conſolation of free agency in the choice of religious opinions, remarkably contributed to the creation of new political energy among all ranks

of

of men, but particularly among the middling and lower claſſes of the people, who by religious controverſy were made, as it were, artificial members of ſociety, and felt the inexpreſſible and captivating delight of think-ing and acting for themſelves, and of touching and affecting general ſociety.—The clergy, irritated to madneſs by the diſ-ſolution of their magic ſuperſti-tion, and looking forward to the total deſtruction of their profit-able fable of the church, perſe-cuted the thinking and reform-

ing

ing people; and this laid the foundation of that perception of religious liberty, which immediately connected itself with political liberty in Scotland so early as the reign of James V, and in England towards the end of the reign of Queen Elizabeth.

Buchanan arose in Scotland like the morning star, to announce the approach of philosophical day.

He was the father of whiggery *as a system* in Britain, if not in Europe; the Lord Bacon or Newton of political science and fentiment, by far the greateft man of his age, as Napier was of his country, in invention: in as much as political fcience is above all others in real importance, with refpect to which we may fairly fet down every other with an adject of a " haud fimile aut fecundum." To women, fome how or other, we have been indebted from the beginning for fortunate revolutions, faving in the cafe of Lady Adam, and even that is not carbonified by the ftricteft theologians.

To the beauty, gaiety, and

im-

imprudence of Mary Stuart, the daughter of James V. we are indebted for the present state of Britain, such as it is. Had Mary been prudent, Scotland might have become a Popish monarchy. England at best would have been under its old monarchy (with proper address), under the Stuarts; and we should not have had occasion to deprecate Gallic freedom with the monstrous infanity of modern Englishmen; but to deplore the want of it.

It were needless and superfluous for me in this sketch to

 deli-

delineate the minute progreſs of puritanical patriotiſm, from the depoſition of Mary Queen of Scots, to that of her great grand-ſon James the Seventh of Scotland, and Second of England.

In Scotland, even down to the period of the union of the kingdoms and parliaments, the people had no nerves for feeling political ſentiment, ſave through the medium of religion or ſuperſtition.

Give Sawney his Sunday's miniſter to his liking, and he cared not who were miniſters

of

of ftate. Even during the long paper as well as cartridge war in the laft century, we hear and fee little in their acts or writings that favoured in the leaft of moral or political liberty. Every thing fmelt of the fcarlet lady of Rome. There were Scottifh Hampdens, but no Sidneys. Buchanan and Fletcher alone were elevated above the ages in which they lived, and fhed a luftre towards thofe that were to fucceed, which will continue to fhine more and more unto the perfect day. I glory in being the attire-

man

man of the characters of such *figurative princes,* and rejoice to think that even in that humble connection my name may be handed down to distant posterity! My anceſtor Marr was a favourite pupil of Buchanan's, imbibed his ſcience and principles, and handed them down to the race of the Stuart Erſkines. I glory alſo, therefore, in paying this family tribute to that glorious pedagogue.

III. I proceed now with pleaſure to the age of philoſophical politics, which Thomſon, my

favourite

favourite bard, and the bard of liberty, faw before his death, like another prophet from Pifgah, faw and rejoiced!

The act of parliament which put an end to the heretable jurifdictions in Scotland, together with the wife and prudent adminiftration. of Archibald Duke of Argyl, and Lord Milton, gave Scotland a free avenue to political and civil exertion: the land was fallow, and cultivated by honeft and active hufbandmen, it prefently bore abundant harvefts. It would be invidious in

my

my own times to select names for enumeration and eulogy. They whom I have formerly named and celebrated will *not* be saved from oblivion by my feeble efforts. They would have lived without my encomium. Yet I arrogate to myself some degree of praise that I was taught, and that I learnt how to discriminate tinsel from gold. Hume, and Napier, and Fletcher, and Buchanan, and Thomson, will live for ever. Can I enough regret that Hume was a tory, and a foolish enthusiast in scepticism?

Yet

Yet I will not attempt to touch his immortality; *my* shafts would but rebound from *his* seven-fold shield. To the divine influence of the *printing-press* is the world indebted for the reign of philosophy; and to philosophy it owes the principles of legislation.

It is with infinite regret that I cannot pretend to produce from Scotland, during this halcyon reign of philosophy, any great character since the death of Fletcher; for Thomson was a retired man, and quite out of the walk of political eminence.

What

What could be expected from a country, where the hereditary members of parliament were impotent, and fearfully queſtioned each other on the diſſolution of a parliament, who were named to be of the ſixteen repreſentatives of the nobility of the country and nation? I beheld this infamous degradation of gentlemen, for I will not ſpeak of noblemen, with diſguſt. I called upon the electors to rouſe from their baneful lethargy; and they thought I was about to raiſe a third rebellion. Yet I perſevered.

vered. By and by they began to leap the fold: they found their account in it; and they also perfevered. But I will fay no more about *them*: liberty, and Buchanan, and Fletcher, and Thomfon, are better themes, or at leaft better fuited to my humble genius.

I ftop rather to enquire concerning the comparative ftate of Britain, in this philofophical age of political fentiment, with France and other countries, that have had inferior advantages.

Who but a clerk of the treafury,

fury, or a lord of the king's bed-chamber, can contemplate this parallel without regret?

It was in the laſt war of George II. that Great Britain laid herſelf under the neceſſity of defending her wide-extended dominion; and of aſſerting her claim to be the firſt nation upon earth. The conteſt was bloody and expenſive, but the end was glorious—The enemy proſtrate and breathleſs, empire extended, honour maintained, peace eſtab-liſhed, and, like the ſun riſing after a ſtorm, a young and na-

tive

tive monarch holding the scep-
tre, and ascending the throne,
amidst the acclamations of the
freest and happiest people on the
globe.

These acclamations are heard
no more. A system of corruption, established and digested
early in this reign *by a baneful
aristocracy*, has pervaded every
rank and order of men, till the
spirit of the constitution has
fled, and left only the *caput
mortuum* behind. The forms of
our government have out-lasted
the ends for which they were

D

insti-

inſtituted, and have become a mere mockery of the people for whoſe benefit they ſhould operate.

The prophecy of Monteſquieu is fulfilled; and nothing can ſave the country but the fulfilment of the prophecy of Franklin. What that prophecy was, what this prophecy is, I leave to the curious to learn. What I have written, I have written: futurity will determine the truth of my own particular predictions, and whether I am to be remembered as a captious

Cynic,

Cynic, or a wife and Pythonic politician.

To conclude: As I think it unneceffary to delineate the fpirit of the times in Europe with refpect to government, fo I think it to be indifpenfably required at my hands, that I fhould, with refpect to Scotland, deprecate the refufal of a militia to my country, the neceffity for which was fo eloquently fet forth by my favourite Fletcher.

That I fhould mark with my blackeft coal the game licence act, which is an infidious and

dan-

dangerous difarming of the commons.

That I fhould exprefs my utter deteftation and abhorrence of the conduct of a firft minifter, who calling himfelf the minifter of the crown, with a treafonable audacity fhould dare to advife the diffolution of a parliament, againft the fenfe of a houfe of commons, the only legal organ of the voice of the people, let that houfe be ever fo ill conftructed, and demand ever fo much reformation.

That

That I fhould loudly pro-
teft, that a parliament ought to
be allowed to die a natural
death. And,

That if a parliament, contem-
plating the foreboding, the ominous imperfections of the conftitution, fhould on its death-
bed provide for a remedy by the
equalization of the reprefenta-
tion of the people, it would
prevent the dangerous concuf-
fion which muft undoubtedly
arife, *and that quickly*, from
their political franchifes being
brought to the level of fur-

round-

rounding nations with a violent jerk. Let us not (said my admirable preceptor and friend, Adam Smith, author of the Esfay on the Wealth of Nations) rafhly believe that Great Britain is capable of fupporting any burden.

Let us confider what hold we have *now* of the two Indies, of Canada, and our other lucrative dependencies. A blow may be ftruck, a blow will be ftruck, that fhall reach the vitals of public credit, and it is an event which nothing but poli-

political infanity can induce
public minifters not to provide
againft.   But no provifion can
be made againft this event, except that which has been pointed out by the finger of the
genius of Britain's welfare.

I will not offer incenfe to
the living, but to the dead: I
infcribe this and the following
fheets to the memory of Sir
George Savile, of Rufford
Hall, Member of Parliament
for the County of York.

D 4

THE
LIFE
OF
ANDREW FLETCHER
OF SALTOUN.

By D. S. EARL OF BUCHAN.

Among innumerable falfe, unmov'd,
Unfhaken, unfeduc'd, unterrify'd,
Nor number, nor example with him wrought
To fwerve from truth, or change his conftant mind,
Though fingle.

PARADISE LOST, b. v.

L I F E

THE
LIFE
OF
ANDREW FLETCHER
OF SALTOUN.

WHEN I did myself the honour, with the affiftance of the learned profeffor Minto, to offer to the public an account of the life, writings, and difcoveries of the inventor of the logarithms, I pledged myfelf to attempt the biography of Fletcher of Saltoun, and of John Law of Laurieston: but when I fet myfelf to the work, I found it much more difficult than I had imagined.

I confefs

I confefs that I am ambitious of permanent reputation, and loath to hazard even the little I may have obtained in promoting that of others, by obtruding on the world what might be brought forward by men of fuperior abilities. But, feveral years having elapfed without my having any profpect of being anticipated, I have yielded to the impulfe of my efteem for the character of Fletcher.

I am afraid, however, that this monument which I endeavour to raife to the memory of my patriotic countryman may induce me to write too freely upon the fubjects which excited my defire to perpetuate his name: but whether I may pleafe or offend the prefent little world of the day, when I decently exprefs the feelings of my heart, or the refult of my reflections, it will give me little concern.

I am

I am the creature of a day, but not the creature of the times.

In politics I would be a Diogenes; and if patronifed by the great Alexander of modern politics, whoever may affect that character, I fhould defire him, as my only requeft, that he would ftand out of my light, that I might behold the beautiful fabric of a free conftitution, undazzled by the fplendour of power, and unintoxicated by the opinion of the people.

Andrew Fletcher of Saltoun was the fon of Sir Robert Fletcher of Saltoun and Innerpeffer, by Catharine Bruce, daughter of Sir Henry Bruce of Clackmannan. By his paternal defcent he was of a family truly honourable, and by his maternal, of the royal race of Bruce; the patriarch of the family of Clackmannan having been the third fon of Robert de Bruce, lord of Annandale, grandfather of

Robert

Robert de Bruce, king of the Scots. His father was the fifth in lineal defcent from Sir Bernard Fletcher of the county of York *. He married Catharine Bruce in the year 1651; and his eldeft fon Andrew, the fubject of my enquiry, was born in the year 1653 †.

When he had the misfortune to lofe his father, he was but in his early youth, and was deftined by his father, on his death-bed, to the care of Dr. Burnet, rector of the parifh of Saltoun, afterwards bifhop of Salifbury, well known

* Sir Robert's father Andrew was one of the fenators of the College of Juftice in Scotland, by the ftyle of Lord Innerpeffer. He was one of thofe feven truly magnanimous Scots who, with David Lord Cardrofs, protefted againft the delivery of King Charles I. at Newcaftle, to the Englifh Parliament. He died 1650.—MS. hift. of the family in my poffeffion.

† MS. hift. ut fupra.

by

by his political zeal and interesting writings. From Burnet he received, as might
have been expected, a very pious and
learned education, and was strongly im-
bued with erudition and the principles of
a free government, which were con-
genial to the family of Fletcher, and es-
poused by his mother, and by those who
had, with her, the charge of his nur-
ture *.

. When he had completed his course of
elementary studies in Scotland, under the
care of his excellent preceptor, he was
sent to travel on the continent.

He was from his infancy of a very
fiery and uncontroulable temper; but his
dispositions were noble and generous †.

* MS. hist. ut supra.

† MS. hist. ut supra; from which, where not dif-
tinguished by other reference, I shall draw all my
authorities.

He

He became firſt known as a public ſpeaker and a man of political energy, being commiſſioner in the Scotch parliament for the ſhire of Eaſt Lothian, when the Duke of York was lord commiſſioner, connecting himſelf with the Earl of Argyll in oppoſition to the Duke of Lauderdale's adminiſtration, and the arbitrary deſigns of the court, which obliged him to retire firſt into England to conſult with Dr. Burnet, and afterwards, by his advice, into Holland. He was ſummoned to appear before the Lords of the Council at Edinburgh, which he not thinking it prudent for him to do, he was outlawed, and his eſtate confiſcated.

In the year 1683 he, with Robert Baillie of Jerviſwood, came into England in order to concert meaſures with the friends of freedom in that country; and

they,

they, I believe, were the only Scotchmen who were admitted into the fecrets of Lord Ruffel's Council of Six. They were likewife the only perfons in whom the Earl of Argyll confided in Holland the common meafures of the two countries, which were then concerted with much fecrecy and danger, for the recovery of the conftitution and liberties of the Britifh kingdoms.

Fletcher managed his part of the negociation with fo much addrefs and prudence, that Adminiftration, though in no refpect delicate as to the means of reaching the objects of their jealoufy or refentment, could find no pretext for feizing him, nor could they fix upon him any of the articles of impeachment for which Mr. Baillie of Jervifwood was condemned and fuffered capital punifhment. Mr.

Baillie was offered his pardon on condition of impeaching his friend Fletcher; but he perfifted to the gallows in rejecting the propofal with indignation. O noble, excellent, and truly worthy Scot! May your defcendants and your countrymen ever remember and imitate your example!

On Fletcher's return to the continent, finding no profpect of his fafe return to Britain, he dedicated his leifure to foreign travel, and to the ftudy of public law and politics; during which period of his life I have fruitlefsly fought for letters that might not only have traced him in his various fituations, but furnifhed agreeable and ufeful materials for his biography.

In the beginning of the year 1685 Fletcher came to the Hague, to affift at the deliberations of the exiles from Britain, and particularly with thofe of his own country, with a view to promote the caufe of oppofition to the arbitrary meafures of James II : but it does not appear that he poffeffed much of the confidence of the party. He was unaccommodating, and ran extravagantly on the project of fetting up a commonwealth in Scotland, or at leaft a monarchy fo limited as hardly to bear any refemblance to a kingdom. His foul was fired with the recollection of the great fpirits that had been raifed by the Greek republics, and, like all men of great abilities, he wifhed for that ftate of things which might mark the fuperiority of his own talents, and give full exercife to his popular powers. Argyll's expedition concerted at that time with Monmouth and the party was the moft inviting to Fletcher ; but being diffatisfied with the plan of operations, and

E 2

his

his countrymen, who enjoyed Monmouth's confidence, he went with the Duke, who was the dupe of the ambitious and crafty Prince of Orange *.

Burnet,

* The ambitious and crafty Prince of Orange.] It is with reluctance that I affix such epithets to a prince who seems to be, as it were, the idol of whigs, who, in hyperbolifing the immortal memory of Old Glorious, feem to forget that he was a man, and a politician. My grandfather and great-grandfather came over with him at the Revolution; and I know that I am not without partiality to a character connected with the eftablifhment of what we call the Conftitution of the country, and with the illuftration of my own family: but I cannot be blind to his faults, nor do I think it would be conducive to the eftablifhment of a real conftitution of freedom in the Britifh nation, that fuch blindnefs fhould continue among the people who wifh to arrange themfelves under the banners of Britifh liberty. That he was ambitious in the difagreeable appli-

cation

Burnet, in the History of his Own Times, informs us that Fletcher had told him,

cation of that epithet appears from his lulling the slumbers of royal security in England, when he was fanning the flames of insurrection against his father-in-law in Holland: from his encouraging the mad project of Monmouth to get him out of the way to the throne, while he was giving good advice to James that the invasion might be defeated. That he was craftily ambitious, appears not only from this double plot, but from his forcing his way to the throne, instead of accepting the regency, by intimidating the chiefs who had invited him over, with a threat of returning to Holland, and leaving them in the hands of an enraged bigoted monarch. That he was ambitious, crafty, and machiavelian, appears from his having given instructions *to take care* of King James, if he should remain at Rochester, and not be disposed to leave the kingdom. Of the wretched device to shake the confidence of the people with respect to the Queen's pregnancy, and the Prince of Wales's birth, I shall say nothing. It

E 3

is

him, that Monmouth, though a weak young man, was sensible of the imprudence of his adventure, and hesitated till he was urged by the party, most of whom were certainly in concert with the Prince of Orange, and considered him as the only probable instrument for dethron-

is the disgrace of the party, and ought to be buried, if possible, in oblivion. It is a dangerous as well as a wicked thing for a prince to take such methods of insuring success, as William himself afterwards found, by the intrigues of the Princess Sophia to turn him out: the proofs of which intrigues King William tied up together in a bundle, which was found in his cabinet. They were seen in Lord Rochford's hands while secretary of state, were afterwards in other hands that need not be mentioned, and were probably treated as heretics were formerly, and as republicans are now wished to be by some other kings. The bundle was docketted by William's own hand—" *Letters of the Princess Sophia to turn me out.*"

ing

ing the king, and fupplanting William in his views, if the attempt were delayed till the Englifh nation fhould become defperate enough to overlook the doubts that Charles II. had confirmed by his declaration in council of the legitimacy of the Duke of Monmouth*. So well was this plot laid, that few of the party in Holland joined in thefe expeditions, but waited either in or out of the fecret, till they fhould fee the effects of the explofion that was to bury poor Monmouth under its

---

* Thofe men urged him on to war and danger, by an appeal to his perfonal courage. They wifhed in this manner to remove a dangerous rival out of the way of the prince's ambition; well-knowing that if the people of England fhould become defperate, they might be induced to overlook the doubts of Monmouth's legitimacy, which had been confirmed by the public declaration of Charles II.

E 4   ruins.

ruins. But Fletcher of Saltoun had neither coolnefs nor fufficient political fubtlety to conduct himfelf with a view to his own private emolument.   Fired by the hopes of a revolution that, from the infignifi-cancy of Monmouth, and the circum-ftances of his birth, might produce a con-ftitution of government in which his re-publican talents might have full fcope, he at firft fell in warmly with the fcheme of Monmouth's landing ; but afterwards, fuf-pecting probably the intrigue of the Prince of Orange, he wifhed it to be laid afide. He told Bifhop Burnet (which fupports this conjecture), that Monmouth was pufhed on to it againft his own fenfe and rea-fon, and was picqued upon the point of honour in hazarding his perfon with his friends.   Monmouth landed at Lime in Dorfetfhire.   Soon after their landing,

Lord

Lord Grey was fent with a fmall party to difperfe a few of the militia, and ran for it; but his men ftood, and the militia retreated. Lord Grey brought back a falfe report, which was foon contradicted by the men, whom their leader had abandoned, coming back to quarters in good order. The unfortunate Duke of Monmouth was ftruck with this (fays Burnet), when he found that the perfon on whom he depended moft, and for whom he defigned the command of the cavalry, had already made himfelf infamous by his cowardice. He intended to join Fletcher with him in that command *: but Fletcher having been fent out on another party, engaged in a fcuffle, in which he had the misfortune to kill the mayor of

* Burnet.

Lynn

Lynn againſt the laws of war, in the ſudden heat of paſſion, on account of contumelious language uſed to him by the mayor, on reclaiming a horſe of his that had been impreſſed by Fletcher's party. This unguarded, unſoldierly, and unjuſtifiable act of violence, muſt have rendered his future ſervices on the expedition of little conſideration to Monmouth; but it was not the cauſe of his leaving the little army. The account given by Fletcher himſelf of his general conduct at this time to the late Earl Marſhall of Scotland, was, that he had been induced to join the Duke of Monmouth, on the principles of the Duke's manifeſtoes in England and Scotland, particularly by the laws promiſed for the permanent ſecurity of civil and political liberty, and of the proteſtant religion, and the calling of a general con-

greſs

grefs of delegates from the people at large, to form a free conftitution of government, and not to pretend to the throne upon any claim, except the free choice of the reprefentatives of the people. That, when Monmouth was proclaimed king at Taunton, he faw his deception, and refolved to proceed no farther in his engagements, which he confidered from that moment as treafon againft the juft rights of the nation, and treachery on the part of Monmouth. That, finding himfelf therefore no longer capable of being ufeful, he left Taunton, and embarked on board a veffel for Spain. That foon after his landing he was committed to prifon; and, on the application of the Englifh minifter at Madrid, he was ordered to be delivered up, and tranfmitted to London in a Spanifh veffel, which was named for that purpofe.

That

That one morning, as he was looking pen-
fively through the bar of his dungeon, he
was accofted by a venerable perfon, who
made fign to fpeak to him. Fletcher, looking if any paffage could be found for his
efcape, difcovered a door open, at which he
was met by his deliverer, with whom he
paffed unmolefted through three guards
of foldiers, who were faft afleep ; and,
without being permitted to return thanks
to his guide, he profecuted his efcape
with the aid of a perfon who feemed to
have been fent for that purpofe, concerning whom he never could obtain any in-
formation. That difguifed he proceeded
in fafety through Spain, where, when he
found himfelf out of all apparent danger,
he lingered, and amufed himfelf with the
view of the country, and with ftudy in
the conventual libraries ; and having pri-
vately

vately obtained credit by bills upon Amsterdam, he bought many rare and curious books, some of which are preserved in the library at Saltoun, in the county of Haddinton. That he had made several very narrow escapes of being detected and seized in the course of his peregrinations through Spain, particularly in the neighbourhood of a town (the name of which Lord Marshall had forgotten), where he intended to have passed the night; but in the skirts of a wood a few miles distant from thence, upon entering a road to the right, he was warned by a woman of a very respectable appearance, to take the left-hand road, as there would be danger in the other direction. Upon his arrival he found the citizens alarmed by the news of a robbery and murder on the road against which he had been cautioned. Some time after this

escape,

efcape, Fletcher's active genius led him to ferve as a volunteer in the Hungarian war *, where he diftinguifhed himfelf by his gallantry and military talents. But the glory which he might have acquired in arms, had he ferved long enough to have obtained a command, he cheerfully facrificed to the fafety of his country.

Perfuaded that the liberties of Britain, if not of all Europe, hung upon the iffue of the defign then in contemplation at the Hague for a revolution in England, and having learned that it had already attained a confiderable degree of maturity, he haftened to Holland, and joined himfelf to the groupe of his countrymen who were attached to the interefts of the Prince of Orange, moft of whom were refugees from England or Scotland. Lord Stair,

* MS. ut fupra.

Lord

Lord Melville, Sir Patrick Hume of Polwarth, Lord Cardrofs, Sir Robert Steuart of Coltnefs, Dr. Burnet, Mr. James Stuart, afterwards lord advocate of Scotland, and Mr. Cunningham, the editor of Horace, and author of a Latin Hiftory of Great Britain, which has been lately tranflated by Dr. W. Thomfon, continuator of principal Watfon's Hiftory of Spain, and author of feveral Philofophical Romances, &c. &c. and publifhed by Dr. Hollingberry, one of the prefent king's chaplains, were the Scots with whom he was in the greateft habits of intimacy *. With thefe gentlemen Fletcher

* Though I hold in fovereign contempt the infignificance of modern anecdote, I fhall fet down in this place fome particulars relating to thefe men, that are characteriftic of their times and hiftories, that may not be unacceptable to the public. Sir Patrick Hume of Polwarth, grandfather of the prefent

chef affociated; but his political principles
were too high and refined, and his fenti-
nients

fent Earl of Marchmont, from his firft appearance
in the Scotch parliament, in the year 1665, as member for the county of Betwick, had diftinguifhed
himfelf by a noble zeal for the liberties of his country. He was the ableft man of the party in oppofition to the adminiftration of the worthlefs Lauderdale; and in the year 1675, when, according to the
defpotic fyftem of that fcandalous engine of the
court, the Scotch privy council, the houfes of perfons
difagreeable to adminiftration were made barracks of
for the troops, he had the fpirit to bring a complaint
into the courts of juftice with refpect to the gar-
rifoning the houfe of Blanfe in Berwickfhire; for the
exercife of which right he was brought before the
privy council, who declared him incapable of all public
truft, committing him prifoner to the common tol-
booth or jail of Edinburgh, where he underwent a
long and tedious imprifonment, from whence, upon
petition on account of ficknefs, he was conveyed to
the caftle of Dunbarton, and afterwards to Stirling
caftle,

ments were too Roman, or rather, as I

may now fay, too Gallic, and too much

in

caftle, where he remained fome years. When libe-

rated, he retired into England, where being in ftrict

habits of friendfhip with the friends of liberty, and

particularly with Lord Ruffel, he found it neceffary

for him to go abroad on the breaking out of the

Rye-houfe plot, and lived fome time at Geneva,

from whence he went to the Hague, to concert

with his fellow-fufferers the meafures that were fol-

lowed by the expeditions of Monmouth and Argyll,

with the latter of whom he came over, and narrowly

efcaped being taken after the defeat of Argyll's

forces, taking fhelter and lying in concealment in

the houfe of the Laird of Langfhaw, and afterwards

in the aifle of the church of Polwarth, the burial-

place of his family. All his food was brought to

him in the night time by his eldeft daughter, then

only twelve years old. This place of concealment

having been difcovered, a party was fent to appre-

hend him. As the foldiers paffed near a gentle-

F   man's

in the odour of philofophical politics, to
accept of the privilege granted by James
the

man's houfe in the neighbourhood, who was friendly
to Sir Patrick, and to liberty, they were invited by
him, who knew their errand, to caroufe on his ale
and beft cheer; while he, aware of the danger of
writing, immediately fent a feather inclofed in a
bit of paper, as a fymbol of flight, to Sir Patrick in
the aifle at Polwarth; who, prefently interpreting the
figure, took horfe, and fortunately efcaped and fled
into Holland, where he remained under the feigned
name of Brown, till he came over with the Prince
of Orange at the Revolution.

Sir Patrick was born on the 13th of January
1641; appointed lord chancellor of Scotland May
2d, 1696; lord high commiffioner, or lord lieutenant
of Scotland, 1702. He died at Berwick on the 1ft
of Auguft 1724, in the 84th year of his age, highly
refpected for his attachment to the liberties of his
country, for his virtue, religion, and learning. His
fon and heir Alexander, Earl of Marchmont, after

a feries

the Second's act of indemnity to return
to his country and eftate, when under the

dominion

a feries of political fituations, not coming as one
does now-a-days from being a fchool-boy to be a
prime minifter, was our ambaffador at the congrefs
of Cambray in the year 1721; and his fon Hugh,
now Earl of Marchmont, made a brilliant figure in
the Houfe of Commons in oppofition to the corrupt
adminiftration of Sir Robert Walpole, and was afterwards an ufeful member of the Houfe of Peers, yet
moft of all diftinguifhed by his learning, and by
having been the friend of Pope, Swift, Atterbury, and
Arbuthnot. Party politics in England cannot fecure
permanent fame; and I rejoice to think that my old
good friend, the friend of my father and grandfather, has fecured his immortality by literature.

In his philofophic retreat at Hemel Hempfted, he
may perhaps deign to be flattered with my hereditary regard.

Henry Lord Cardrofs, the fon of David Lord
Cardrofs of Dryburgh, &c. who protefted againft

                                        he

dominion of difguifed defpotifm, fancti-
fied by a venal parliament: fo that

when

the delivering up of King Charles I. at Newcaftle,
had been trained, in the manner of his family, in
the exalted principles of religion, liberty, and learning; and early joined himfelf to the oppofers of the
Duke of Lauderdale's adminiftration. For his lady's
hearing her own chaplain preach in her own houfe,
he was fined in five thoufand pounds, of which he
paid a thoufand; and, after many months attendance
at court for procuring a difcharge of the overplus of
his fine, was finally imprifoned in the caftle of Edinburgh, where he continued four years; while his
houfe of Cardrofs in Perthfhire, immediately after
it had been repaired, and furnifhed at a great expence, was garrifoned to his great lofs and vexation.
And in June 1679, the king's forces, in their march to
the weft (the day before the Duke of Buccleugh came
to them), wheeled and went about two miles out of
the road, that they might quarter on Lord Cardrofs's
eftates of Kirkhall and Uphall, in Weft Lothian.

After-

when Argyll, Sutherland, Melville, and others had recovered their inheritances in

Afterwards, having obtained his liberation, he went to North America, and eftablifhed a colony in Carolina, which was deftroyed by the Spaniards. He returned, broken but not difpirited by misfortunes, to Europe, and attached himfelf to the friends of liberty in Holland. He raifed a regiment of dragoons, on the Revolution, and was an ufeful commander under M'Kay in Scotland, in fubduing the remains of oppofition there to the new government; but died of the effects of his fufferings, in the year 1693, in the 43d year of his age.—Concerning Sir Robert Steuart of Coltnefs, there is an anecdote fo hiftorically curious, that I cannot pafs him over without notice, though he was a perfon of no extraordinary eminence. In the end of the year 1686, when the bufinefs of the Teft was in agitation, William Penn was employed at the court of the Prince of Orange, to reconcile the Stadtholder to the views of his father-in-law. Penn became acquainted with moft.

In the year 1686, he chofe rather to remain in exile than to accept of liberty

as

of the Scotch fugitives, and, among the reft, with
Sir Robert Steuart, and his brother James, who
wrote the famous Anfwer to Fagel's Memorial, and
will be mentioned more particularly hereafter: and
finding that the violence of their zeal reached little
farther than the enjoyment of their religious liberty,
on his return to London he advifed the meafure of
an indemnity and recal to the perfecuted Prefbyterians, who had not been engaged in treafonable
acts of oppofition to the civil government. Sir
Thomas availed himfelf of this indemnity to return
to his own country; but found his eftate and only
means of fubfiftence in the poffeffion of the Earl of
Arran, afterwards Duke of Hamilton. Soon after
his coming to London he met Penn, who congra-
tulated him on his being juft about to feel experi-
mentally the pleafure fo beautifully expreffed by
Horace, of the " Mihi me reddentis agelli." Coltnefs
fighed, and faid, " Ah, Mr. Penn! Arran has got

my

as a royal favour!   Yet Alexander Cunningham, the hiftorian, though a Whig and

my eftate, and I fear my fituation is about to be now worfe than ever."   "What do you fay, Gofpel?" (a name Coltnefs had got at the Hague :) "You furprife and grieve me exceedingly.   Come to my houfe to-morrow, and I will fet matters to rights for thee."

Penn went immediately to Arran.   "What is this, friend James," faid he to him, "that I hear of thee? Thou haft taken poffeffion of Coltnefs's eftate; thou knoweft that it is not thine."   "That eftate," replied Arran, "I paid a great price for.   I received no other reward for my expenfive and troublefome embaffy in France except this eftate; and I am certainly much out of pocket by the bargain."

"All very well, friend James," faid the Quaker; "but of this affure thyfelf, that if thou doft not give me this moment an order on thy chamberlain for two hundred pounds to Coltnefs, to carry him down to his native country, and a hundred a year to fubfift on till matters are adjufted, I will make it as

and friend of Fletcher, mentions this conduct of Fletcher's as extravagant. It was reserved for this age of wonders to exhibit the true principles of political sentiment, unconnected with superstition and personal attachment to kings or to parties.

Fletcher made a manly, noble appear-

many thousands out of thy way with the king." Arran instantly complied, and Penn sent for Sir Robert, and gave him the security. After the Revolution, Sir Thomas, with the rest, had full restitution of his estate, and Arran was obliged to account for all the rents he had received; against which this payment only was allowed to be stated.—This authentic particular I received from my illustrious uncle, the late Sir James Steuart Denham, father of the present worthy member for Clydesdale. It strongly marks the keenness of King James to facilitate his foolish measures in favour of his religion and arbitrary power.

ance

ance in that convention which met in Scotland, after the Revolution, for the settlement of the new government. In Scotland the rights and liberties of the people had been determined and fixed by multiplied instances of changing the order of succession, and attainting their sovereigns for treason against the rights of the people: and it is to Scotland and a Scotchman that the world is indebted for the establishment of the philosophical and logical principles of a free constitution both in theory and practice. George Buchanan, the greatest man of his age, as well as country, established, by irrefragable arguments, in his treatise or dialogue concerning the rights of the people of Scotland, the rights of all mankind; was the father of whiggery, and, what is much grander, the father of that system

which

which will one day verify the prophecies of the Chriftian Scriptures, to the abafe-ment of kings, and the deftruction of prieftcraft.

Raymond de Sebonde in France, the friend of Montaigne, adopted the prin-ciples of Buchanan in his Lettre fur la Ser-vitude Volontaire, a beautiful little piece publifhed by his friend, which being uni-verfally read with the Effays of Mon-taigne, kept up the facred fire of freedom in France, in the midft of folly and defpo-tifm, till the progrefs of commerce, print-ing, philofophy, and literature opened the eyes of Frenchmen every where to difcover that they were men, and ought to be citizens; that men were not born with *gold chains* about their necks, with ftars' upon their breafts, or coronets upon their heads; that it is of the nature of kings

as

as hitherto conftituted, to confider their interefts as feparate from their nations, and to watch continually like wolves or foxes for their prey, in order to deftroy the citizens committed to their charge; that it is neceffary, therefore, that they fhould have only the power of obeying the laws made by the people, with that of doing good; but that the power of doing mifchief, either by prerogative or *influence*, ought to be taken away. Thefe were the principles of Fletcher, principles that feemed extravagant, difloyal, and impracticable in his days; but which are now acknowledged almoft every where, except in Spain, Germany, and England. Thefe have ever been the principles of his biographer: but he will not ftoop to examine the ravings of a fublime and

beautiful

4

beautiful apologift for tyranny and fuper-

ftition.

> " A fairer perfon loft not heaven ; he feem'd
> For dignity compos'd, and high exploit :
> But all was falfe and hollow ; though his tongue
> Dropp'd manna, and could make the worfe appear
> The better reafon, to perplex and dafh
> Matureft counfels."

A man formed like Cicero for finging like a nightingale in a cage, to be kept for the gratification of luxurious patricians, now the friend of Pompey, and now of Cæfar, as it fuited the indulgence of his inordinate vanity ; fond of words like a fchool-mafter, and fond of trappings like a filly little girl let out of a boarding-fchool. I would indulge him with a copy of verfes of my own compofition, written in the ftyle of a madrigal upon my mif-trefs's eye-brow.

" Mould'ring

" Mould'ring and frail, to duft the body tends,
And human greatnefs ftubborn fortune bends :
Fleeting and vain the ftoried urns arife,
And like a cloud the human vapour flies.
Vain are our bufts and portraits to retain
The foul's bright form, and light the lamp again :
By life alone the mimic form revives,
A Tully dead, a Tully yet furvives ;
Mortal by nature, endlefs in the kind,
Succeffive ages fhew the kindred mind."

Fletcher ufed to fay with Cromwell and Milton, that the trappings of a monarchy and a great ariftocracy would patch up a very clever little commonwealth. Being in company one day with the witty Dr. Pitcairn, the converfation turned on a perfon of learning whofe hiftory was not diftinctly known. " I knew the man well," faid Fletcher: "he was hereditary profeffor of divinity at Hamburgh." " *Hereditary* profeffor!" faid Pitcairn, with

a laugh

a laugh of aftonifhment and derifion.
"Yes, Doctor," replied Fletcher, "hereditary profeffor of divinity. What think
you of a hereditary king?"

Having faid fo much upon the principles of Fletcher, I think it proper at this
juncture of political reform in Europe,
that I fhould guard my own expreffed
opinions againft popular mifinterpretation
on a fubject of fuch great importance to
the happinefs of my country.

I have ever thought it was a misfortune
to Britain that the Revolution was followed by fo imperfect a fyftem of political
arrangement, and that it would have been
more conducive to the future happinefs
of the nation, if we had had to erect an
entire new fabric of a conftitution in the
prefent improved ftate of fociety, than to
clear out, patch, and buttrefs the edifice,

as

as has been partially done by the Convention Parliament in the year 1689, by the Bill of Rights, by the Act of Succession, by the Treaty of Union, by the abolition of heritable jurisdictions and feudal tenures, of personal slavery, the confirmation and extension of the act of Habeas Corpus, the security of the liberty of speech and writing, and of printing, the securing private property against the claims and nullum tempus of the crown, the abridgment of the powers of the ecclesiastical courts, the abolition of personal slavery in Britain, the independency of the salaries of the criminal and civil judges and magistrates, by the Grenvilian law of elections, the exclusion of tax-gatherers from the right of popular suffrage in elections of members of parliament, and finally by the declaration of

the

the rights of juries, as judges both of the law and of the fact.

But as things are now fituated, Britain muft be fatisfied to fall at leaft a century behind all other nations, that, like America and France, have had the advantage of erecting a conftitution from the firft foundations of jurifprudence, and of efcaping the dangers that arife from dilapidation.

Had I a crazy old family manfion, I fhould have been better pleafed that my fathers had left me the tafk of erecting a new one, which I might have done cheaper and better than patching the old; but having the manfion, I fhould confider well before I pulled it to the ground. The conftitution of England, Scotland, and Ireland admits of a great and a fafe improvement, which will be foon demanded and obtained by the people, the

equalization

equalization of the rights of election, and the abolition of the rights of primogeniture in private fucceffion. But I would warn my countrymen againft every approach to hafty determination upon the methods of repairing the old houfe, left it fhould tumble about their ears.

When the fanatics, in the year 1567, came to pull down the cathedral of Glafgow, a gardener who ftood by, faid, "My friends, cannot you make it a houfe for ferving your God in your own way? For it would coft your country a great deal to build fuch another." The fanatics defifted, and it is the only cathedral in Scotland, that remains entire and fit for fervice. Such, therefore, with refpect to the Britifh conftitution, is the advice of the gardener of Dryburgh Abbey. I reject the uniform as I do the principles

of

of the Windsor Club, nor will I give any preference to that of Carleton-House, where sense and reason are out of the question: but I unaffectedly write in sincerity and truth, what I know to be conducive to the tranquillity and future happiness of a prosperous and industrious, but corrupted and enervated people.

It was said of Fletcher, that he wished for a republic in which he himself should rule by his popular talents; but his temper was unaccomodating: nor is there any ground for supposing that his views in any transaction were selfish. He was the contriver and mover of the act of the Scotch parliament to stop any settlement of the crown until the constitution was formed, and the rights of the people secured; and his speeches on that occasion will be found in this volume, full of

good

good fenfe, and of manly claffical eloquence.

The Duke of Hamilton was fufpected
of wifhing to embarrafs the fettlement of
the crown, with a view to favour the
eventual pretenfions of his own family.
He went fecretly on board the fhip of
Van Aärfen Somelsdijke, the Dutch admiral in the road of Leith, and propofed an union of Scotland and Holland
as one commonwealth. It may be gueffed
who expected to be vice ftadtholder in
Scotland *. Nothing could be more natural than the averfion the Scots felt to
be funk and loft in the great empire of
Britain; and it was as natural for Hamilton and Fletcher to foment this averfion
with different intentions, and from differ-

* Communicated by Somelsdijke to his relation
Lord Auchenleck, one of the fenators of the College
of Juftice in Scotland.

G 2

ent

ent motives.   Lockhart of Carnwath, the memoir writer, flattered himfelf that Fletcher was a Tory, if not a Jacobite, in his heart, becaufe he affociated with Tories and Jacobites; but he did not reflect that the Tories and Jacobites were then the country party, and that Fletcher would hear more from them of the dignity, independence, and intereft of his country, and lefs about a king that infpires a republican with no fentiment but terror or diflike.   This, I believe, was the foundation for his being fufpected *of not being a true Whig at bottom*; for Whigs and Tories were in thofe days quite diftinct, difliking and avoiding each other, not mingled together as they now are, to fhare among themfelves the plunder of their country.

From the moft minute examination
of

of the records and memoirs of the times, it fufficiently appears, that while others, whether Whigs or Tories, were endeavouring to turn the Revolution in Britain to the promoting of their own felfifh purpofes, Fletcher neither afked nor obtained any emolument from the court; but that he was continually attentive to the intereft and honour of Scotland.

When an attempt was made, in the year 1692, to bring about a counter-revolution, Fletcher's ruling principle (though diffatisfied with King William) was the good of his country. He ufed all his influence with the Duke of Hamilton to forget the caufes of his difguft, and to co-operate with the friends of a free conftitution *.

* Vide Fletcher's Letter to the Duke, Dalrymple's Memoirs.

In

In every propofal for the happinefs and glory of his country, Fletcher was interefted as if it tended to his own perfonal emolument and reputation. He was the firft friend and patron of that extraordinary man Paterfon, the projeétor of the Darien Company; to whofe merits my kinfman Sir John Dalrymple has done the juftice they deferve, in the laft volume of his interefting Memoirs of Great Britain, which, unable as I am to defcribe with equal fpirit and ability the fhare Fletcher had in this bufinefs, I fhall give in Sir John's own words.

" Ingenious men draw to each other like iron and the loadftone : Paterfon, on his return to London, formed a friendfhip with Mr. Fletcher of Saltoun, whofe mind was inflamed with the love of pub-

lic good, and all of whofe ideas to procure it had a fublimity in them. Fletcher
difliked England merely becaufe he loved
Scotland to excefs; and therefore the report common in Scotland is probably
true, that he was the perfon who perfuaded Paterfon to truft the fate of his
project to his own countrymen alone,
and to let them have the fole benefit,
glory, and danger in it; for in its danger
Fletcher deemed fome of its glory to con-
fift. Although Fletcher had nothing to
hope for, and nothing to fear, becaufe he
had a good eftate, and no children; and
though he was of the country party; yet
in all his fchemes for the public good, he
was in ufe to go as readily to the king's
minifters as to his own friends, being indifferent who had the honour of doing

G 4

good,

good, provided it was done. His houfe of Saltoun in Eaſt Lothian was near to that of the Marquis of Tweedale, then miniſter for Scotland; and they were often together. Fletcher brought Paterſon down to Scotland with him, prefented him to the Marquis, and then, with that power which a vehement ſpirit always poſſeſſes over a diffident one, perſuaded the Marquis, by arguments of public good, and of the honour which would redound to his adminiſtration, to adopt the project. Lord Stair and Mr. Johnſton, the two fecretaries of ſtate, patroniſed thoſe abilities in Paterſon which they poſſeſſed in themſelves; and the lord advocate, Sir James Steuart, the fame man who had adjuſted the Prince of Orange's declaration at the Revolution, whoſe ſon was

married

married to a niece of Lord Stair *, went naturally along with his connections."

———————

FROM this busy period till the meeting of the Union Parliament, Fletcher

* Anne Dalrymple, daughter of Sir Hugh Dalrymple, lord president of the Court of Session, was married to Sir James Steuart of Goodtrees, baronet, solicitor general for Scotland, and by him was the mother of the late learned and truly eminent Sir James Steuart Denham, author of the Principles of Political Oeconomy; and four daughters, the second of whom, Agnes, of elegant taste and genius, was the mother of all my father's children, some of whom inherit her abilities, the strong natural parts and probity of the father, with the taste and brilliant imagination of the mother. " Fortes creantur fortibus & bonis." If this compliment to my brothers shall appear too strong, and be blamed, I look for the reward of Proculeius —" Notus in fratres animi paterni."

was

was uniform and indefatigable in his par-
liamentary conduct, continually attentive
to the rights of the people, and *jealous,
as every friend to his country ought to
be, of their invasion by the king and his
ministers ; for it is as much of the nature
of kings and ministers to invade and destroy the rights of the people, as it is of
foxes and weasels to rifle a poultry yard,
and destroy the poultry.*—All of them
therefore ought to be muzzled.

Fletcher was accordingly a strenuous but
unfuccefsful advocate for a national militia.
His difcourfe on that important fubject
written at this time, was not printed until the year 1698. In this Difcourfe he
fays, what I wifh I had a voice loud
enough to be heard over all Britain and
Ireland, to rattle in the ears of the people—" A good and effective militia is of

fuch

such importance to a nation, that it is the chief part of the conſtitution of any free government. For though, as to other things, the conſtitution be ever ſo ſlight, a good militia will always preſerve the public liberty. But in the beſt conſtitution that ever was, as to all other parts of government, if the militia be not upon a right foot, the liberty of that people muſt periſh.

" The Swiſs," ſays he, " at this day are the freeſt, happieſt, and the people of all Europe who can beſt defend themſelves, becauſe they have the beſt militia."

What a reproach to the nobility, the gentry, and to the people of Scotland, is it not, that, attending to the dirty conſi-deration of pleaſing a ſub-miniſter of Scot-

land,

land, they should have lately flinched from forcing the British legislature to make them free citizens, and to enjoy the free use of arms in defence of their own constitution!

———Pudet hæc opprobria nobis,
Et dici potuisse, & non potuisse refelli!

In the year 1703 we find Fletcher great in the debates concerning the fixing the succession to the crown of Scotland, in the event of Queen Anne's dying without issue; which he strenuously and successfully urged the parliament to determine before they should think of granting any supplies to the crown. It was even resolved, that the successor to the crown after Queen Anne, should not be the same person that was King or Queen of England, *unless the just rights of Scotland* should be declared in parliament at London,

don, and fully fettled independent of English interefts and councils; and what is remarkable, that wife and excellent, but feemingly very ftrong rule of the French conftitution, that the king or queen fhould *not* have the power of engaging the nation in war without the confent of parliament, was determined upon by the parliament of Scotland; in the fupport and preparation of which law, and others for the fecurity of Scottifh freedom, Mr. Fletcher had a confiderable fhare, and had great influence by the power of his fervent and manly eloquence. " Prejudice and opinion," faid he, " govern the world, to the great diftrefs and ruin of mankind; and though we daily find men fo rational as to charm by the difinterefted rectitude of their fentiments in all other things, yet, when we touch upon any wrong opinion of theirs

with

with which they have been early prepossessed, we find them more irrational
than any thing in nature, and not only
not to be convinced, but obstinately resolved not to hear any reason against it.
These prejudices are yet stronger when
they are taken up by great numbers of
men, who confirm each other through
the course of several generations, and seem
to have their blood tainted, or, to speak
more properly, their animal spirits influenced by them. Of these delusions, one
of the strongest and most pernicious has
been a violent inclination in many men
to extend the prerogative of the prince to
an absolute and unlimited power. And
though in limited monarchies all good
men profess and declare themselves enemies to all tyrannical practices, yet many
even of these are found ready to oppose

such

such neceſſary limitations as might ſecure them from the tyrannical exerciſe of power in a prince, not only ſubject to all the infirmities of other men, but, by the temptations ariſing from his power, to far greater. This *humour* * has increaſed greatly in the Scottiſh nation, ſince the union of the crowns in 1603; and the ſlaviſh ſubmiſſions, which have been made neceſſary to procure the favours of the court, have cheriſhed and fomented a ſlaviſh principle. I muſt put the repreſentatives of the Scots in mind, that no ſuch principles were known in this kingdom before the union of the crowns, *and that no monarchy in Europe* was more limited, nor any

---

* *Humeur*, Scoto-Gallic, fancy, whim. An oppreſſed people can never know what the Engliſh exhibited of humour *when they were free.*

people

people more jealous of liberty than the Scots *."

Fletcher

* I David Stewart, Earl of Buchan, do throw this gauntlet of Fletcher's down, in the prefence of all England; and if any man fhall take it up, I will try my ftrength with him; but I will not argue with women or priefts, till I fhall fee them leaving their trenches of petticoats and fuperftition, and meeting me on the fair and manly field of hiftorical know‑ledge.

Hume told the people of England the truth about their old conftitution, and they called him a Tory. I tell them that Hume was in the right, and I defy them to call *me* a Tory. It was no rarity for the Scots to dethrone a King for attacking the liberties of the people. They difmiffed Baliol becaufe he fold his country; they difmiffed Mary becaufe fhe meant to govern them like the France of the Guifes; they brought in Bruce as the Prince of Orange of Scotland; and for the principles and practice I refer to Buchanan's Dialogue de Jure Regni apud Scotos.

There

Fletcher was by far the moſt nervous and correct ſpeaker in the parliament of Scotland,

There never was ſuch a thing as a peer of Scotland. There were earls indeed, but they did not ſit in parliament in right of their earldoms, but in right of their lands; and there they were only on a par with other proprietors of fiefs. James I. of the Scots indeed attempted to introduce the Engliſh modes, and was murdered, like Cæſar, by his kinſ-man; and James VI. by the ſtatute 1587, introduced the practice of the election of repreſentatives for the freeholders; but the nobility, as they were called, *not the peerage* of Scotland, were no more than the barons or freeholders, barons of baron-rent, who by uſage retained their privilege of ſitting in parliament in right of their lands, which if they ſold, they loſt their right of ſitting, along with their poſſeſſions.

There was but one houſe of parliment: and in this, unfortunately for Scotland, the prieſts had a privilege to ſit in right of their lands. But the Scots had no notion of ſuch a monſtrous organ of power for their king, as a ſeparate houſe for his ſervants

H

and

Scotland, for he drew his style from the pure models of antiquity, and not from the grosser practical oratory of his contemporaries; so that his speeches and his language will bear a comparison with the best speeches of the reign of Queen Anne, the Augustan age of Great Britain, far superior to the meretricious, inflated, metaphorical style of our modern orators; from which remark I must set down Mr. Charles Fox, member for Westminster in the present parliament, as a wonderful exception. In many respects Fox re-

and chaplains, to stop the progress of laws in favour of the rights of the people, before they should come to receive the royal assent. As to the idea of a perfect constitution being to consist of three parts, this was a trinity in which the Scots did not believe; and they satisfied themselves with holding the doctrine of the unity, the majesty, and uncontroulable power of the legislative authority.

sembles

fembles Fletcher; and may he clofe his career fo as to deferve an equal character!

. The irafcibility of Fletcher's temper, and his high fenfe of honour, made him impatient of the flighteft tendency towards an affront. Lord Stair, when fecretary of ftate, having let fall fome expreffions in parliament, that feemed to glance at Fletcher, he feized Stair by the robe, in his place, and gave him the reply valiant. Lord Stair was called to order by the Houfe, and was obliged to afk his pardon publicly.

Fletcher's fpeeches on the confideration of the Treaty of Union being printed in the following fheets of this volume, I fhall only quote a paffage of Alexander Cunningham's hiftory, relating to his appearances on that important occafion. " Andreas Fletferus, ut qui patriam prius in libertatem vindicaret, bis se in vitæ discrimen intulerat, nunc vulnus infanabile reipublicæ inferendum, et Scotiam veluti funere per suos elatam, cernens hoc tempore extremo, in dicendo effervescit, reginæque ministros vehementer infectatur, et exagitat, nihil res domesticas, licet amplas, faciens. Sunt qui illius vim eloquentiæ, etiam in inimicitiis gerendis, virtutem nimium efferbuisse, & causæ nocuisse dicunt; *sed quid vetat filium in funere matris commoveri*, aut civem fortem, in efferendam funere patriam, dolore graviter inuri, præsertim is qui reipublicæ commoda suis necessitudinibus semper potiora duxerat, mortemque pro patria toties oppetere non dubitaverat? Buchaniæ etiam comes ejusq; patruus Joannes Areskinus strenue pro patria contende-

bant,

bant, *nihil penfi cum Galliæ factionis ho-
minibus habentes."*

Fletcher (fays the anonymous author
of his character in Thomas Rawlinfon's
library) was fteady in his principles, of
nice honour, great learning; brave as
the fword he wore; a fure friend, but an
irreconcileable enemy; and would not
do a bafe thing to efcape death.

He would not fubmit to be called either
Whig or Tory, faying, *thofe names were
given and ufed to cloak the knaves of both
parties.*   Bravo!

He had acquired the grammatical knowledge of the Italian fo perfectly as to
compofe and publifh a treatife in that
language; yet he could not fpeak it, as he
found when having an interview with
Prince Eugene of Savoy, and being ad-

                 dreffed

dreſſed in that language by the Prince, he could not utter a ſyllable to be under-ſtood. In his perſon he was of low ſtature, thin, of a brown complexion, with piercing eyes; and a gentle frown of keen ſenſibility appeared often upon his countenance.

To the memory of this extraordinary man I have reared this monument. The bodies of men are frail and periſhing : ſo are their portraits and monuments : but, upheld by the power of the Creator, the form of the ſoul is eternal. This cannot be repreſented by ſtatues or by pictures, nor otherwiſe than by a con-formity of manners. May whatever was great and truly valuable in Fletcher be for ever imitated by my countrymen, and may the ſplendour of his virtues re-

flect

flect honour upon his family, and glorify his kindred throughout all generations!

Ille ego qui quondam patriæ perculſus amore
Civibus oppreſſis libertati ſuccurrere auſim,
Nunc arva paterna colo, fugioq; limina regum.

Dryburgh Abbey,
July 14, 1791.

APPENDIX,

THE family of Fletcher of Saltoun descends from Sir Bernard Fletcher, a son of Fletcher of Hatton in the county of Cumberland. Robert, his son, established himself in the county of Tweedale. Andrew, the son of Robert, was a merchant at Dundee, in the county of Angus or Forfar. David, the son of Andrew, purchased the estate of Innerpeffer in that county, and married a daughter of Ogilvie of

Pourie,

Pourie, and by her had three sons, Robert, Andrew, and David. Robert died 1613, leaving six sons: Andrew; James, provost of Dundee; Robert, laird of Bencho; Sir George Fletcher of Restenet in Angus-shire; and two others, who died in infancy. Andrew was knighted by James I. 1620; the same year he succeeded his father in the estate of Innerpeffer. He bought the estate of Saltoun in East Lothian, in the year 1643, which had anciently given title to the Lords Abernethy of Saltoun, now represented by the Frasers of Cowie and Philorth, Lords Abernethy of Saltoun. He was one of the senators of the College of Justices in Scotland, by the title of Lord Innerpeffer, as has been mentioned in the life of his grandson; as well as his noble dissent from the surrender of Charles I. to the English army at Newcastle, with Lord

.4   Cardross

Cardrofs and others; who thought the king deferved to be punifhed, but not by thofe to whom he had entrufted the care of his protection.

Lord Innerpeffer was the father of Sir Robert Fletcher of Saltoun, who was the father of the patriot.

With refpect to Fletcher's character in forfaking the Duke of Monmouth at Taunton, the following teftimony of Fergufon, in a MS. quoted by Echard, in his Hiftory of England, ought to be well weighed and confidered before Fletcher be charged with unallowable defertion.

" The Duke of Monmouth was very fenfible of his precipitous adventure into England; but fuffered himfelf to be over-ruled, contrary to both the dictates of his judgment,

judgment, and the bias of his inclination; for could he have been allowed
to have purfued his own fentiments
and refolutions, he intended to have
fpent that fummer in the court of
Swedeland. But from this he was di-
verted by the importunity of the Earl of
Argyll, and prevailed upon by the advice
and intreaty of the Lord Grey and Mr.
Wade (*contrary to the defires of Mr. Fletcher, and Captain Matthews*) to haften
into England. To which I can fay (faith
Mr. Fergufon) I had the leaft acceffion of
any, who were about the Duke of Monmouth. Nor would the Earl of Argyll,
after his own *ominous* hafte, fet fail for
Scotland, till he forced a promife from
the Duke of embarking for England within fo many days after. Which the Duke,
rather than fuffer his honour to be ftained,

complied

complied with as far as weather would permit; though he found the obferving his word to interfere with his intereft, as well as all the principles of prudence and difcretion."—My tendernefs for the ad-mirers of King William, and my regard for the illuftrious houfe of Campbell, will not allow me to exprefs what I fufpect in the whole of this tranfaction in Hol-land. Argyll paid the amende honor-able with a vengeance. And the defcen-dants of Monmouth need not regret the cowardice and perjury of Charles II. nor the failure of poor Monmouth's attempt. It is remarkable that the heir of Mon-mouth is now the eventual heir general of that very Earl of Argyll, who precipi-tated the ruin of his patriarch.

SPEECHES

SPEECHES of Mr. FLETCHER

On the QUESTION for the

SETTLEMENT

OF THE

SCOTTISH CROWN,

Delivered in the Scottish Parliament, 1703.

My Lord Chancellor,

I AM not surprised to find an act for a supply brought into this house at the beginning of a session. I know custom has, for a long time, made it common. But, I think, experience might teach us, that such acts should be the last of every session; or lie upon the table, till all other great affairs of the nation be finished, and then only granted. It is a strange pro-

position

pofition which is ufually made in this houfe; that if we will give money to the crown, then the crown will give us good laws: as if we were to buy good laws of the crown, and pay money to our princes, that they may do their duty, and comply with their coronation oath. And yet this is not the worft; for we have often had promifes of good laws, and when we have given the fums demanded, thofe promifes have been broken, and the nation left to feek a remedy; which is not to be found, unlefs we obtain the laws we want, before we give a fupply. And if this be a fufficient reafon at all times to poftpone a money-act, can we be blamed for doing fo at this time, when the duty we owe to our country indifpenfably obliges us to provide for the common fafety in cafe of an event, altogether out

of

of our power, and which muſt neceſſarily diſſolve the government, unleſs we continue and ſecure it by new laws; I mean the death of her majeſty, which God in his mercy long avert? I move, therefore, that the houſe would take into conſideration what acts are neceſſary to ſecure our religion, liberty, and trade, in caſe of the ſaid event, before any act of ſupply, or other buſineſs whatever be brought into deliberation.

Act concerning offices, &c. brought in by the ſame member.

'THE eſtates of parliament taking 'into their conſideration, that, to the 'great loſs and detriment of this nation, 'great ſums of money are yearly carried

I   'out

‘ out of it, by thofe who wait and depend
‘ at court, for places and preferments in
‘ this kingdom : and that by Scotfmen,
‘ employing Englifh intereft at court, in
‘ order to obtain their feveral pretenfions,
‘ this nation is in hazard of being brought
‘ to depend upon Englifh minifters : and
‘ likewife confidering, that by reafon our
‘ princes do no more refide amongft us,
‘ they cannot be rightly informed of the
‘ merit of perfons pretending to places,
‘ offices, and penfions; therefore our fo-
‘ vereign lady, with advice and confent
‘ of the eftates of parliament, ftatutes and
‘ ordains, that after the deceafe of her
‘ majefty, whom God long preferve, and
‘ heirs of her body failing, all places and
‘ offices both civil and military, and all
‘ penfions, formerly conferred by our

kings,

'kings, shall ever after be given by par-
'liament, by way of ballot.'

II.

MY LORD CHANCELLOR,

WHEN our kings succeeded to the crown of England, the ministers of that nation took a short way to ruin us, by concurring with their inclinations to extend the prerogative in Scotland; and the great places and pensions conferred upon Scotsmen by that court, made them to be willing instruments in the work. From that time this nation began to give away their privileges one after the other, though they then stood more in need of having them enlarged. And as the col-

I 2   lections

lections of our laws, before the Union of the Crowns, are full of acts to secure our liberty, those laws that have been made since that time are directed chiefly to extend the prerogative. And that we might not know what rights and liberties were still ours, nor be excited by the memory of what our anceftors enjoyed, to recover thofe we had loft, in the two laft editions of our acts of parliament the moft confiderable laws for the liberty of the fubject are induftriously and defignedly left out. All our affairs fince the Union of the Crowns have been managed by the advice of Englifh minifters, and the principal offices of the kingdom filled with fuch men as the court of England knew would be fubfervient to their defigns: by which means they have had fo vifible an influence upon our whole adminiftration,

that

that we have, from that time, appeared
to the reft of the world more like a con-
quered province, than a free independent
people.   The account is very fhort:
whilft our princes are not abfolute in
England, they muft be influenced by that
nation, our minifters muft follow the
directions of the prince, or lofe their
places, and our places and penfions will
be diftributed according to the inclinations
of a king of England, fo long as a king
of England has the difpofal of them:
neither fhall any man obtain the leaft advancement, who refufes to vote in council
and parliament under that influence.   So
that there is no way to free this country
from a ruinous dependance upon the
Englifh court, unlefs by placing the power
of conferring offices and penfions in the
parliament, fo long as we fhall have the

I 3

fame

fame king with England. The ancient
kings of Scotland, and even thofe of
France, had not the power of conferring
the chief offices of ftate, though each of
them had only one kingdom to govern,
and that the difficulty we labour under,
of two kingdoms which have different
interefts governed by the fame king, did
not occur. Befides, we all know that
the difpofal of our places and penfions is
fo confiderable a thing to a king of England, that feveral of our princes, fince the
Union of the Crowns, have wifhed to be
free from the trouble of deciding between
the many pretenders. That which would
have given them eafe, will give us liberty,
and make us fignificant to the common
intereft of both nations. Without this,
it is impoffible to free us from a dependence on the Englifh court : all other re-

medies and conditions of government will
prove ineffectual, as plainly appears from
the nature of the thing; for who is not
fenfible of the influence of places and
penfions upon all men and all affairs?
If our minifters continue to be appointed
by the Englifh court, and this nation
may not be permitted to difpofe of the
offices and places of this kingdom to balance the Englifh bribery, they will corrupt every thing to that degree, that if
any of our laws ftand in their way they
will get them repealed. Let no man
fay, that it cannot be proved, that the
Englifh court has ever beftowed any
bribe in this country. For they beftow
all offices and penfions; they bribe us,
and are mafters of us at our own coft.
It is nothing but an Englifh intereft in
this houfe, that thofe, who wifh well to

I 4

our

our country have to ftruggle with at this time. We may, if we pleafe, dream of other remedies; but fo long as Scotfmen muft go to the Englifh court to obtain offices of truft or profit in this kingdom, thofe offices will always be managed with regard to the court and intereft of England, though to the betraying of the intereft of this nation, whenever it comes in competition with that of England. And what lefs can be expected, unlefs we refolve to expect miracles, and that greedy, ambitious, and for the moft part neceffitous men, involved in great debts, burdened with great families, and having great titles to fupport, will lay down their places, rather than comply with an Englifh intereft in obedience to the prince's commands? Now, to find Scotfmen oppofing this, and willing that Englifh minifters,

for

for this is the cafe, fhould have the difpofal
of places and penfions in Scotland, rather
than their own parliament, is matter of
great aftonifhment; but that it fhould be
fo much as a queftion in the parliament,
is altogether incomprehenfible: and if an
indifferent perfon were to judge, he would
certainly fay we were an Englifh parliament. Every man knows that princes
give places and penfions by the influence
of thofe who advife them. So that the
queftion comes to no more than, whether
this nation would be in a better condition,
if, in conferring our places and penfions,
the prince fhould be determined by the
parliament of Scotland, or by the minifters
of a court, that make it their intereft to
keep us low and miferable. We all know
that this is the caufe of our poverty, mifery and dependence. But we have been

for

for a long time so poor, so miserable, and depending, that we have neither heart nor courage, though we want not the means, to free ourselves.

III.

My Lord Chancellor,

PREJUDICE and opinion govern the world, to the great distress and ruin of mankind; and though we daily find men so rational as to charm by the disinterested rectitude of their sentiments in all other things, yet when we touch upon any wrong opinion with which they have been early prepossessed, we find them more irrational than any thing in nature; and not only not to be convinced, but obstinately resolved not to hear any reason against it. These prejudices are yet stronger

when

when they are taken up by great numbers of men, who confirm each other
through the courfe of feveral generations,
and feem to have their blood tainted, or,
to fpeak more properly, their animal fpirits
influenced by them. Of thefe delufions,
one of the ftrongeft, and moft pernicious,
has been a violent inclination in many
men to extend the prerogative of the
prince to an abfolute and unlimited power.
And though, in limited monarchies, all
good men profefs and declare themfelves
enemies to all tyrannical practices, yet
many, even of thefe, are found ready to
oppofe fuch neceffary limitations as might
fecure them from the tyrannical exercife
of power in a prince, not only fubject to
all the infirmities of other men, but, by
the temptations arifing from his power,
to far greater. This humour has greatly

increafed

increased in our nation, since the Union of the Crowns; and the slavish submissions, which have been made neceffary to procure the favours of the court, have cherifhed and fomented a flavish principle. But I muft take leave to put the reprefentatives of this nation in mind, that no fuch principles were in this kingdom before the Union of the Crowns; and that no monarchy in Europe was more limited, nor any people more jealous of liberty than the Scots. Thefe principles were firft introduced among us after the Union of the Crowns, and the prerogative extended to the overthrow of our ancient conftitution, chiefly by the prelatical party; though the peevifh, imprudent, and deteftable conduct of the prefbyterians, who oppofed thefe principles only in others, drove many into them, gave them greater

force,

force, and rooted them more deeply in this nation. Should we not be afhamed to embrace opinions contrary to reafon, and contrary to the fentiments of our anceftors, merely upon account of the uncharitable and infupportable humour and ridiculous conduct of bigots of any fort? If then no fuch principles were in this nation, and the conftitution of our government had greatly limited the prince's power before the Union of the Crowns; dare any man fay he is a Scotfman, and refufe his confent to reduce the government of this nation, after the expiration of the intail, within the fame limits as before that union? And if, fince the Union of the Crowns, every one fees that we ftand in need of more limitations; will any man act in fo direct an oppofition to his own reafon, and the un-

doubted

doubted intereſt of his country, as not to concur in limiting the government yet more than before the Union, particularly by the addition of this ſo neceſſary limitation for which I am now ſpeaking? My Lord, theſe are ſuch clear demonſtrations of what we ought to do in ſuch conjunctures, that all men of common ingenuity muſt be aſhamed of entering into any other meaſures. Let us not then tread in the ſteps of mean and fawning prieſts of any ſort, who are always diſpoſed to place an abſolute power in the prince, if he on his part will gratify their ambition, and by all means ſupport their form of church-government, to the perſecution of all other men, who will not comply with their impoſitions. Let us begin where our anceſtors left off before the Union of the Crowns, and be for the

future,

future, more jealous of our liberties, becaufe there is more need. But I muft
take upon me to fay, that he who is not
for fetting great limitations upon the
power of the prince, particularly that for
which I am fpeaking, in cafe we have the
fame king with England, can act by no
principle, whether he be a prefbyterian,
prelatical, or prerogative man, for the
court of St. Germains, or that of Hanover; I fay, he can act by no principle
unlefs that of being a flave to the court
of England for his own advantage. And
therefore let not thofe, who go under
the name of prerogative-men, cover themfelves with the pretext of principles in
this cafe; for fuch men are plainly for
the prerogative of the Englifh court over
this nation, becaufe this limitation is demanded.

manded only in cafe we come to have
the fame king with England.

---

*Act for the fecurity of the kingdom, brought
in by the fame member.*

'THE eftates of parliament confider-
'ing, that when it fhall pleafe God to
'afflict this nation with the death of our
'fovereign lady the queen (whom God of
'his infinite mercy long preferve) if the
'fame fhall happen to be without heirs
'of her body, this kingdom may fall into
'great confufion and diforder before a fuc-
'ceffor can be declared. For preventing
'thereof, our fovereign lady, with advice
'and confent of the eftates of parliament,
'ftatutes and ordains, that if, at the afore-
'faid time, any parliament or convention

of

' of eftates fhall be affembled, then the
' members of that parliament or conven-
' tion of eftates fhall take the adminiftra-
' tion of the government upon them:
' excepting thofe barons and boroughs,
' who, at the aforefaid time, fhall have
' any place or penfion, mediately or im-
' mediately, of the crown: whofe com-
' miffions are hereby declared to be void;
' and that new members fhall be chofen
' in their place: but if there be no parlia-
' ment or convention of eftates actually
' affembled, then the members of the cur-
' rent parliament fhall affemble with all
' poffible diligence: and if there be no
' current parliament, then the members
' of the laft diffolved parliament, or con-
' vention of eftates, fhall affemble in like
' manner: and in thofe two laft cafes, fo
' foon as there fhall be one hundred

K   ' members

‘ members met, in which number the ba-
‘ rons and boroughs before-mentioned are
‘ not to be reckoned, they fhall take the
‘ adminiftration of the government upon
‘ them: but neither they, nor the mem-
‘ bers of parliament or convention of
‘ eftates, if at the time aforefaid affem-
‘ bled, fhall proceed to the weighty affair
‘ of naming and declaring a fucceffor, till
‘ twenty days after they have affumed
‘ the adminiftration of the government:
‘ both that there may be time for all the
‘ other members to come to Edinburgh,
‘ which is hereby declared the place of
‘ their meeting, and for the election of
‘ new barons and boroughs in place above-
‘ mentioned. But fo foon as the twenty
‘ days are elapfed, then they fhall proceed
‘ to the publifhing, by proclamation, the
‘ conditions of government, on which

‘ they

' they will receive the fucceffor to the
' imperial crown of this realm; which,
' in the cafe only of our being under the
' fame king with England, are as follow.

   1. ' That elections fhall be made at
' every Michaelmas head-court for a new
' parliament every year: to fit the firft of
' November next following, and adjourn
' themfelves from time to time, till next
' Michaelmas: that they choofe their own
' prefident, and that every thing fhall be
' determined by balloting, in place of
' voting.

   2. ' That fo many leffer barons fhall
' be added to the parliament, as there
' have been noblemen created fince the
' laft augmentation of the number of the
' barons; and that in all time coming, for
' every nobleman that fhall be created,

K 2

                                              ' there

' there fhall be a baron added to the par-
' liament.

3. ' That no man have vote in par-
' liament but a nobleman or elected
' member.

4. ' That the king fhall give the fanc-
' tion to all laws offered by the eftates ;
' and that the prefident of the parliament
' be impowered by his majefty to give
' the fanction in his abfence, and have
' ten pounds fterling a day falary.

5. ' That a committee of one and
' thirty members, of which nine to be a
' quorum, chofen out of their own num-
' ber, by every parliament, fhall, during
' the intervals of parliament, under the
' king, have the adminiftration of the
' government, be his council, and ac-
' countable to the next parliament ; with

power

' power on extraordinary occasions to
' call the parliament together : and that
' in the said council, all things be deter-
' mined by balloting in place of voting.

6. ' That the king, without consent
' of parliament, shall not have the power
' of making peace and war; or that of
' concluding any treaty with any other
' state or potentate.

7. ' That all places and offices, both
' civil and military, and all pensions for-
' merly conferred by our kings, shall ever
' after be given by parliament.

8. ' That no regiment or company of
' horse, foot, or dragoons, be kept on foot
' in peace or war, but by consent of par-
' liament.

9. ' That all the fencible men of the
' nation, betwixt sixty and sixteen, be,
' with all diligence possible, armed with

K 3

' bayonets,

' bayonets, and firelocks all of a caliber,
' and continue always provided in such
' arms, with ammunition suitable.

10. ' That no general indemnity, nor
' pardon for any transgression against the
' public, shall be valid without consent
' of parliament.

11. ' That the fifteen senators of the
' College of Justice shall be incapable of
' being members of parliament, or of any
' other office, or any pension: but the
' salary that belongs to their place to be
' increased as the parliament shall think
' fit: that the office of president shall be
' in three of their number to be named
' by parliament, and that there be no
' extraordinary lords.   And also, that the
' lords of the justice-court shall be distinct
' from those of the session, and under the
' same restrictions.

12. ' That

12. 'That if any king break in upon any
' of these conditions of government, he
' shall, by the estates, be declared to have
' forfeited the crown.

'Which proclamation made, they are
' to go on to the naming and declaring
' a successor: and when he is declared,
' if present, are to read to him the claim
' of right and conditions of government
' above-mentioned, and to desire of him,
' that he may accept the crown accord-
' ingly; and he accepting, they are to
' administer to him the oath of corona-
' tion: but if the successor be not present,
' they are to delegate such of their own
' number as they shall think fit, to see
' the same performed, as said is: and
' are to continue in the administration
' of the government, until the successor's
' accepting of the crown, upon the afore-

K 4 ' said

‘ said terms, be known to them : where-
‘ upon having then a king at their head,
‘ they ſhall, by his authority, declare them-
‘ ſelves a parliament, and proceed to the
‘ doing of whatever ſhall be thought ex-
‘ pedient for the welfare of the realm. And
‘ it is likewiſe, by the authority aforeſaid,
‘ declared, that if her preſent majeſty
‘ ſhall think fit, during her own time,
‘ with the advice and conſent of the
‘ eſtates of parliament, failing heirs of her
‘ body, to declare a ſucceſſor, yet never-
‘ theleſs, after her majeſty's deceaſe, the
‘ members of parliament or convention
‘ ſhall, in the ſeveral caſes, and after the
‘ manner above ſpecified, meet and admit
‘ the ſucceſſor to the government, in the
‘ terms, and after the manner, as ſaid is.
‘ And it is hereby further declared, that
‘ after the deceaſe of her majeſty, and

‘ failing

' failing heirs of her body, the foremen-
' tioned manner and method shall, in the
' several cases, be that of declaring and
' admitting to the government all those
' who shall hereafter succeed to the im-
' perial crown of this realm: and that it
' shall be high treason for any man to
' own or acknowledge any person as king
' or queen of this realm, till they are
' declared and admitted in the above-
' mentioned manner. And lastly, it is
' hereby declared, that by the death of
' her majesty, or any of 'her successors,
' all commissions, both civil and military,
' fall and are void; and that this act
' shall come in place of the seventeenth
' act of the sixth session of king William's
' parliament. And all acts and laws, that
' any way derogate from this present act,

' are

' are hereby in fo far declared void and
' abrogated.'

IV.

MY LORD CHANCELLOR,

IT is the utmoft height of human prudence to fee and embrace every favourable
opportunity: and if a word fpoken in
feafon does, for the moft part, produce
wonderful effects; of what confequence
and advantage muft it be to a nation in
deliberations of the higheft moment; in
occafions, when paft, for ever irretrievable,
to enter into the right path, and take
hold of the golden opportunity which
makes the moft arduous things eafy, and
without which the moft inconfiderable
may put a ftop to all our affairs? We

have

have this day an opportunity in our hands which if we manage to the advantage of the nation we have the honour to represent, we may, so far as the viciffitude and uncertainty of human affairs will permit, be for many ages eafy and happy. But if we defpife or neglect this occafion, we have voted our perpetual dependence on another nation. If men could always retain thofe juft impreffions of things they at fome times have upon their minds, they would be much more fteady in their actions. And as I may boldly fay, that no man is to be found in this houfe, who, at fome time or other, has not had that juft fenfe of the miferable condition to which this nation is reduced by a dependence upon the Englifh court, I fhould demand no more but the like impreffions at this time to pafs all the limitations

mentioned

mentioned in the draught of an act I have already brought into this houfe; fince they are not limitations upon any prince, who fhall only be king of Scotland, nor do any way tend to feparate us from England; but calculated merely to this end, that fo long as we continue to be under the fame prince with our neighbour nation, we may be free from the influence of Englifh councils and minifters; that the nation may not be impoverifhed by an expenfive attendance at court, and that the force and exercife of our government may be, as far as is poffible, within ourfelves. By which means trade, manufactures, and hufbandry will flourifh, and the affairs of the nation be no longer neglected, as they have been hitherto.

Thefe are the ends to which all the limitations

tations are directed, that Englifh councils may not hinder the acts of our parliaments from receiving the royal affent; that we may not be engaged without our confent in the quarrels they may have with other nations; that they may not obftruct the meeting of our parliaments, nor interrupt their fitting; that we may not ftand in need of pofting to London for places and penfions, by which, whatever particular men may get, the nation muft always be a lofer; nor apply for the remedies of our grievances to a court, where, for the moft part, none are to be had. On the contrary, if thefe conditions of government be enacted, our conftitution will be amended, and our grievances be eafily redreffed by a due execution of our own laws, which to this day we have never been able to obtain. The beft and

wifeft

wifeſt men in England will be glad to hear that theſe limitations are ſettled by us. For though the ambition of courtiers lead them to deſire an uncontroulable power at any rate; yet wiſer men will conſider, that when two nations live under the ſame prince, the condition of the one cannot be made intolerable, but a ſeparation muſt inevitably follow, which will be dangerous if not deſtructive to both. The ſenate of Rome wiſely determined in the buſineſs of the Privernates, that all people would take hold of the firſt opportunity to free themſelves from an uneaſy condition; that no peace could be laſting, in which both parties did not find their account; and that no alliance was ſtrong enough to keep two nations in amity, if the condition of either were made worſe by it. For my own part,

my

my lord chancellor, before I will confent
to continue in our prefent miferable and
languifhing condition after the deceafe of
her majefty, and heirs of her body failing,
I fhall rather give my vote for a ·fe-
paration from England at any rate. · I
hope no man, who is now poffeffed of
an office, will take umbrage at thefe conditions of government, though fome of
them feem to diminifh, and others do entirely fupprefs the place he poffeffes: for
befides the fcandal of preferring a private
intereft before that of our country, thefe
limitations are not to take place immediately. The queen is yet young, and by
the grace of God may live many years, I
hope longer than all thofe fhe has placed
in any truft; and fhould we not be happy,
if thofe who, for the future, may defign
to recommend themfelves for any office,

could

could not do it by any other way than the favour of this houfe, which they who appear for thefe conditions well deferve in a more eminent degree? Would we rather court an Englifh minifter for a place than a parliament of Scotland? Are we afraid of being taken out of the hands of Englifh courtiers, and left to govern ourfelves? And do we doubt whether an Englifh miniftry or a Scots parliament will be moft for the intereft of Scotland? But that which feems moft difficult in this queftion, and in which if fatisfaction be given, I hope no man will pretend to be diffatisfied with thefe limitations, is the intereft of a king of Great Britain. And here I fhall take liberty to fay, that as the limitations do no way affect any prince that may be king of Scotland only, fo they will be found highly advantageous to a king of Great Britain. Some of our late kings, when they have been perplexed about the affairs of Scotland, did let fall such expreſſions as intimated they thought them not worth their application. And indeed we ought not to wonder if princes, like other men, ſhould grow weary of toiling where they find no advantage. But to ſet this affair in a true light: I deſire to know, whether it can be more advantageous to a king of Great Britain to have an unlimited prerogative over this country, in our preſent ill condition, which turns to no account, than that this nation, grown rich and powerful under theſe conditions of government, ſhould be able upon any emergency to furniſh a good body of land forces, with a ſquadron of ſhips for war, all paid by ourſelves, to aſſiſt his majeſty in the wars

L

he

he may undertake for the defence of the proteſtant religion and liberties of Europe. Now, ſince I hope I have ſhewn, that thoſe who are for the prerogative of the kings of Scotland, and all thoſe who are poſſeſſed of places at this time, together with the whole Engliſh nation, as well as a king of Great Britain, have cauſe to be ſatisfied with theſe regulations of government, I would know what difficulty can remain; unleſs that, being accuſtomed to live in a dependency, and unacquainted with liberty, we know not ſo much as the meaning of the word; nor, if that ſhould be explained to us, can ever perſuade ourſelves we ſhall obtain the thing, though we have it in our power, by a few votes, to ſet ourſelves and our poſterity free. To ſay that this will ſtop at the royal aſſent, is a ſuggeſtion diſreſpectful to her majeſty,

and

and which ought neither to be mentioned in parliament, nor be confidered by any member of this houfe. And, were this a proper time, I am confident I could fay fuch things as, being reprefented to the queen, would convince her, that no perfon can have greater intereft, nor obtain more lafting honour, by the enacting of thefe conditions of government, than her majefty. And if the nation be affifted in this exigency by the good offices of his grace the high commiffioner, I fhall not doubt to affirm, that in procuring this bleffing to our country from her majefty, he will do more for us, than all the great men of that noble family, of which he is defcended, ever did; though it feems to have been their peculiar province for divers ages, to defend the liberties of this nation againft the power of the Englifh and the deceit of courtiers. What further arguments can I ufe to perfuade this houfe to enact thefe limitations, and embrace this occafion, which we have fo little deferved? I might bring many; but the moft proper and effectual to perfuade all, I take to be this: that our anceftors did enjoy the moft effential liberties contained in the act I propofed: and though fome few of lefs moment are among them which they had not, yet they were in poffeffion of divers others not contained in thefe articles: that they enjoyed thefe privileges when they were feparated from England, had their prince living among them, and confequently ftood not in fo great need of thefe limitations. Now, fince we have been under the fame prince with England, and therefore ftand in the greateft need of them, we have not only

neglected

neglected to make a due provision of that kind, but in divers parliaments have given away our liberties, and upon the matter subjected this crown to the court of England; and are become so accuftomed to depend on them, that we feem to doubt whether we fhall lay hold of this happy opportunity to refume our freedom. If nothing elfe will move us, at leaft let us not act in oppofition to the light of our own reafon and confcience, which daily reprefents to us the ill conftitution of our government, the low condition into which we are funk, and the extreme poverty, diftrefs, and mifery of our people. Let us confider whether we will have the nation continue in thefe deplorable circumftances, and lofe this opportunity of bringing freedom and plenty among us. Sure the heart of every honeft man muft bleed daily, to

L 3   fee

fee the mifery in which our commons,
and even many of our gentry, live ; which
has no other caufe but the ill conftitution
of our government, and our bad government no other root but our dependence
upon the court of England.   If our kings
lived among us, it would not be ftrange
to find thefe limitations rejeóted.   It is
not the prerogative of a king of Scotland
I would diminifh, but the prerogative of
Englifh minifters over this nation.   To
conclude, thefe conditions of government
being either fuch as our anceftors enjoyed,
or principally direóted to cut off our dependence on an Englifh court, and not to
take place during the life of the queen ;
he who refufes his confent to them, whatever he may be by birth, cannot fure be a
Scotfman by affeótion. This will be a true
teft to diftinguifh, not whig from tory,

7.   prefby-

presbyterian from episcopal, Hanover from St. Germains, nor yet a courtier from a man out of place; but a proper test to distinguish a friend from an enemy to his country. And indeed we are split into so many parties, and cover ourselves with so many false pretexts, that such a test seems necessary to bring us into the light, and shew every man in his own colours. In a word, my lord chancellor, we are to consider, that though we suffer under many grievances, yet our dependence upon the court of England is the cause of all, comprehends them all, and is the band that ties up the bundle. If we break this, they will all drop and fall to the ground: if not, this band will straiten us more and more, till we shall be no longer a people.

I therefore humbly propose, that, for the security of our religion, liberty, and

L 4

trade,

trade, thefe limitations be declared, by a
refolution of this houfe, to be the conditions, upon which the nation will receive a fucceffor to the crown of this
realm, after the deceafe of her prefent majefty, and failing heirs of her body, in
cafe the faid fucceffor fhall be alfo king or
queen of England.

V.

MY LORD CHANCELLOR,

I AM forry to hear what has been juft
now fpoken from the throne. I know the
duty I owe to her majefty, and the refpect that is due to her commiffioner; and
therefore fhall fpeak with a juft regard to
both. But the duty I owe to my country
obliges me to fay, that what we have now
heard from the throne, muft of neceffity

5   proceed

proceed from Englifh councils. If we had demanded, that thefe limitations fhould take place during the life of her majefty, or of the heirs of her body, perhaps we might have no great reafon to complain, though they fhould be refufed.   But that her majefty fhould prefer the prerogative of fhe knows not who, to the happinefs of the whole people of Scotland; that fhe fhould deny her affent to fuch conditions of government as are not limitations upon the crown of Scotland, but only fuch as are abfolutely neceffary to relieve us from a fubjection to the court of England, muft proceed from Englifh councils; as well becaufe there is no Scots minifter now at London, as becaufe I have had an account, which I believe to be too well grounded, that a letter to this effect has been fent down hither by the lord trea-

furer

furer of England, not many days ago.
Befides, all men who have lately been at
London well know, that nothing has been
more common, than to fee Scotfmen of
the feveral parties addreffing themfelves
to Englifh minifters about Scots affairs;
and even to fome ladies of that court,
whom, for the refpect I bear to their relations, I fhall not name. Now, whether
we fhall continue under the influence and
fubjection of the Englifh court; or whether it be not high time to lay before her
majefty, by a vote of this houfe, the conditions of government upon which we
will receive a fucceffor, I leave to the
wifdom of the parliament. This I muft
fay, that to tell us any thing of her majefty's intentions in this affair, before we
have prefented any act to that purpofe for
the royal affent, is to prejudge the caufe,

and

and altogether unparliamentary. I will add, that nothing has ever shewn the power and force of English councils upon our affairs in a more eminent manner at any time, since the union of the crowns. No man in this house is more convinced of the great advantage of that peace which both nations enjoy by living under one prince. But as, on the one hand, some men, for private ends, and in order to get into offices, have either neglected or betrayed the interest of this nation, by a mean compliance with the English court; so on the other side it cannot be denied, that we have been but indifferently used by the English nation. I shall not insist upon the affair of Darien, in which, by their means and influence chiefly, we suffered so great a loss both in men and money, as to put us almost beyond hope

of

of ever having any confiderable trade; and this contrary to their own true intereſt, which now appears but too viſibly. I ſhall not go about to enumerate inſtances of a provoking nature in other matters, but keep myſelf preciſely to the thing we are upon. The Engliſh nation did, ſome time paſt, take into conſideration the nomination of a ſucceſſor to that crown; an affair of the higheſt importance, and, one would think, of common concernment to both kingdoms. Did they ever require our concurrence? Did they ever deſire the late king to cauſe the parliament of Scotland to meet, in order to take our advice and conſent? Was not this to tell us plainly, that we ought to be concluded by their determinations, and were not worthy to be conſulted in the matter? Indeed, my lord chancellor, conſidering

—   their

their whole carriage in this affair, and the broad infinuations we have now heard, that we are not to expect her majefty's affent to any limitations on a fucceffor (which muft proceed from Englifh councils), and confidering we cannot propofe to ourfelves any other relief from that fervitude we lie under by the influence of that court; it is my opinion, that the houfe come to a refolution, *That after the deceafe of her majefty, heirs of her body failing, we will feparate our crown from that of England.*

VI.

MY LORD CHANCELLOR,

THAT there fhould be limitations on a fucceffor, in order to take away our dependence on the court of England, if both

nations

nations fhould have the same king, no man here feems to oppofe. And I think very few will be of opinion, that fuch limitations fhould be deferred till the meeting of the nation's reprefentatives upon the deceafe of her majefty. For if the fucceffor be not named before that time, every one will be fo earneft to promote the pretenfions of the perfon he moft affects, that new conditions will be altogether forgotten. So that thofe who are only in appearance for thefe limitations, and in reality againft them, endeavour for their laft refuge to miflead well-meaning men, by telling them, that it is not advifable to put them into the act of fecurity, as well for fear of lofing all, as becaufe they will be more conveniently placed in a feparate act. My lord chancellor, I would fain know if any thing can be

more

more proper in an act which appoints the naming and manner of admitting a fucceffor, than the conditions on which we agree to receive him.   I would know, if the deferring of any thing, at a time when naturally it fhould take place, be not to put a flur upon it, and an endeavour to defeat it.   And if the limitations in queftion are pretended to be fuch a burden in the act, as to hazard the lofs of the whole, can we expect to obtain them when feparated from the act ?   Is there any common fenfe in this ?   Let us not deceive ourfelves, and imagine that the act of 1696 does not expire immediately after the queen and heirs of her body; for in all that act, the heirs and fucceffors of his late majefty king William are always reftrained and fpecified by thefe exprefs words, ' ac
' cording to the declaration of the eftates,
' dated

' dated the 11th of April 1689.' So that,
unlefs we make a due provifion by fome
new law, a diffolution of the government
will enfue immediately upon the death of
her majefty, failing heirs of her body.
Such an act therefore being of abfolute
and indifpenfable neceffity, I am of opinion, that the limitations ought to be in-
ferted therein as the only proper place
for them, and fureft way to obtain them:
and that whoever would feparate them,
does not fo much defire we fhould obtain
the act, as that we fhould lofe the limitations.

VII.

MY LORD CHANCELLOR,

I HOPE I need not inform this honourable houfe, that all acts which can be propofed

pofed for the fecurity of this kingdom, are vain and empty-propofitions, unlefs they are fupported by arms; and that to rely upon any law, without fuch a fecurity, is to lean upon a fhadow. We had better never pafs this act: for then we fhall not imagine we have done any thing for our fecurity; and if we think we can do any thing effectual without that provifion, we deceive ourfelves, and are in a moft dangerous condition. Such an act cannot be faid to be an act for the fecurity of any thing, in which the moft neceffary claufe is wanting, and without which all the reft is of no force; neither can any kingdom be really fecured but by arming the people. Let no man pretend that we have ftanding forces to fupport this law; and that, if their numbers be not fufficient, we may raife more. It is very well known

M   this

this nation cannot maintain fo many ftanding forces as would be neceffary for our
defence, though we could entirely rely
upon their fidelity. The poffeffion of arms
is the diftinction of a freeman from a
flave. He who has nothing, and belongs
to another, muft be defended by him, and
needs no arms: but he who thinks he is
his own mafter, and has any thing he
may call his own, ought to have arms to
defend himfelf and what he poffeffes, or
elfe he lives precarioufly and at difcretion.
And though for a while thofe who have
the fword in their power abftain from
doing him injuries; yet, by degrees, he
will be awed into a fubmiffion to every arbitrary command. Our anceftors, by being
always armed, and frequently in action,
defended themfelves againft the Romans,
Danes, and Englifh; and maintained their

liberty

liberty againſt the incroachments of their own princes. If we are not rich enough to pay a ſufficient number of ſtanding forces, we have at leaſt this advantage, that arms in our own hands ſerve no leſs to maintain our liberty at home, than to defend us from enemies abroad. Other nations, if they think they can truſt ſtanding forces, may, by their means, defend themſelves againſt foreign enemies, But we, who have not wealth ſufficient to pay ſuch forces, ſhould not, of all nations under heaven, be unarmed. For us then to continue without arms, is to be directly in the condition of ſlaves: to be found unarmed, in the event of her majeſty's death, would be to have no manner of ſecurity for our liberty, property, or the independence of this kingdom. By being unarmed, we every day run the riſk of our

all,

all, fince we know not how foon that event may overtake us: to continue ftill unarmed, when, by this very act now under deliberation, we have put a cafe, which happening may feparate us from England, would be the groffeft of all follies. And if we do not provide for arming the kingdom in fuch an exigency, we fhall become a jeft and a proverb to the world.

***

VIII.

MY LORD CHANCELLOR,

IF in the fad event of her majefty's deceafe without heirs of her body, any confiderable military force fhould be in the hands of one or more men, who might have an underftanding together, we are not very fure what ufe they would make

of

of them in so nice and critical a conjunc-
ture. We know, that as the most just and
honourable enterprises, when they fail,
are accounted in the number of rebellions;
so all attempts, however unjust, if they
succeed, always purge themselves of all
guilt and imputation. If a man presume
he shall have success, and obtain the utmost
of his hopes, he will not too nicely examine the point of right, nor balance too
scrupulously the injury he does to his
country. I would not have any man take
this for a reflection upon those honourable persons, who have at present the
command of our troops. For, besides
that we are not certain who shall be in
those commands at the time of such an
event, we are to know that all men are
frail, and the wicked and mean-spirited
world has paid too much honour to many,

M 3

who

who have subverted the liberties of their
country. We see a great disposition at this
time in some men, not to consent to any
limitations on a successor, though we
should name the same with England.
And therefore since this is probably the
last opportunity we shall ever have of
freeing ourselves from our dependence on
the English court, we ought to manage it
with the utmost jealousy and diffidence
of such men. For though we have ordered the nation to be armed and exer-
cised, which will be a sufficient defence
when done; yet we know not but the
event, which God avert, may happen before this can be effected. And we may
easily imagine, what a few bold men, at
the head of a small number of regular
troops, might do, when all things are in
confusion and suspense. So that we ought

to make effectual provifion, with the utmoft circumfpection, that all fuch forces may be fubfervient to the government and intereft of this nation, and not to the private ambition of their commanders. I therefore move, that immediately upon the deceafe of her majefty, all military commiffions above that of a captain be null and void.

IX.

My Lord Chancellor,

I KNOW it is the undoubted prerogative of her majefty, that no act of this houfe fhall have the force of a law without her royal affent. And as I am confident his grace the high commiffioner is fufficiently inftructed, to give that affent to

 every

every act which fhall be laid before him;
fo more particularly to the act for the fecurity of the kingdom, which has already
paffed this houfe: an act that preferves us
from anarchy: an act that arms a de-
fencelefs people: an act that has coft the
reprefentatives of this kingdom much time
and labour to frame, and the nation a very
great expence: an act that has paffed by a
great majority: and above all, an act that
contains a caution of the higheft importance for the amendment of our conftitution. I did not prefume the other day,
immediately after this act was voted, to
defire the royal affent; I thought it a juft
deference to the high commiffioner, not
to mention it at that time. Neither would
I now, but only that I may have an opportunity to reprefent to his grace, that as he
who gives readily doubles the gift; fo his

grace

grace has now in his hands the moft glorious and honourable occafion, that any perfon of this nation ever had, of making himfelf acceptable, and his memory for ever grateful to the people of this kingdom: fince the honour of giving the royal affent to a law, which lays a lafting foundation for their liberties, has been referved to him.

X.

MY LORD CHANCELLOR,

ON the day that the act for the fecurity of the kingdom paffed in this houfe, I did not prefume to move for the royal affent. The next day of our meeting, I mentioned it with all imaginable refpect and deference, for his grace the high commiffioner,

miffioner, and divers honourable perfons
feconded me. If now, after the noble
lord who fpoke laft, I infift upon it, I
think I am no way to be blamed. I fhall
not endeavour to fhew the neceffity of
this act, in which the whole fecurity of
the nation now lies, having fpoken to
that point the other day: but fhall take
occafion to fay fomething concerning the
delay of giving the royal affent to acts
paffed in this houfe; for which I could
never hear a good reafon, except that a
commiffioner was not fufficiently inftructed. But that cannot be the true
reafon at this time, becaufe feveral acts
have lain long for the royal affent: in
particular, that to ratify a former act,
for turning the convention into a parliament, and fencing the claim of right,
which no man doubts his grace is fuffi-

ciently

ciently inftructed to pafs. We muft therefore look elfewhere for the reafon of this delay, and ought to be excufed in doing this; fince fo little regard is had, and fo little fatisfaction given to the re-prefentatives of this nation, who have for more than three months employed them-felves with the greateft affiduity in the fer-vice of their country, and yet have not feen the leaft fruit of their labours crowned with the royal affent. Only one act has been touched, for recognizing her majefty's juft right, which is a thing of courfe. This gives but too good reafon to thofe who fpeak freely, to fay that the royal affent is induftrioufly fufpended, in order to oblige fome men to vote, as fhall be moft expedient to a certain intereft; and that this feffion of parliament is continued fo long, chiefly to make men uneafy, who

have

have neither places nor penfions to bear
their charges; that by this means acts
for money, importation of French wine,
and the like, may pafs in a thin houfe,
which will not fail immediately to receive the royal affent, whilft the acts that
concern the welfare, and perhaps the
very being of the nation, remain un- .
touched.

XI.

MY LORD CHANCELLOR,

BEING under fome apprehenfions that
her majefty may receive ill advice in this
affair, from minifters who frequently mif-
take former bad practices for good pre-
cedents, I defire that the third act of the
firft feffion of the firft parliament of king
Charles the Second may be read.

Act

Act the third of the first session, Par. I.
Car, II.

Act asserting his majesty's royal prerogative,
in calling and dissolving of parliaments,
and making of laws.

'THE estates of parliament, now con-
' vened by his majesty's special authority,
' considering that the quietness, stability,
' and happiness of the people, do depend
' upon the safety of the king's majesty's
' sacred person, and the maintenance of
' his sovereign authority, princely power,
' and prerogative royal; and conceiving
' themselves obliged in conscience, and
' in discharge of their duties to almighty
' God, to the king's majesty, and to their
' native country, to make a due acknow-
' ledgment thereof at this time, do there-
' fore unanimously declare, that they will,

' with

' with their lives and fortunes, maintain
' and defend the fame. And they do
' hereby acknowledge, that the power of
' calling, holding, proroguing, and dif-
' folving of parliaments, and all conven-
' tions and meetings of the eftates does
' folely refide in the king's majefty, his
' heirs and fucceffors. And that as no
' parliament can be lawfully kept, without
' the fpecial warrant and prefence of the
' king's majefty, or his commiffioner;
' fo no acts, fentences or ftatutes, to be
' paffed in parliament, can be binding
' upon the people, or have the authority
' and force of laws, without the fpecial
' authority and approbation of the king's
' majefty, or his commiffioner interponed
' thereto, at the making thereof. And
' therefore the king's majefty, with ad-
' vice and confent of his eftates of parlia-
' ment,

‘ ment, doth hereby refcind and annul all
‘ laws, acts, ftatutes, or practices that have
‘ been, or upon any pretext whatfoever
‘ may be, or feem contrary to, or incon-
‘ fiftent with, his majefty’s juft power
‘ and prerogative above-mentioned; and
‘ declares the fame to have been unlaw-
‘ ful, and to be void and null in all
‘ time coming. And to the end that
‘ this act and acknowledgment, which
‘ the eftates of parliament, from the fenfe
‘ of their humble duty and certain know-
‘ ledge, have hereby made, may receive
‘ the more exact obedience in time coming;
‘ it is by his majefty, with advice afore-
‘ faid, ftatute and ordained, that the punc-
‘ tual obfervance thereof be fpecially re-
‘ garded by all his majefty’s fubjects, and
‘ that none of them, upon any pretext
‘ whatfoever, offer to call in queftion, im-

pugn,

' pugn, or do any deed to the contrary
' hereof, under pain of treason.'

My Lord Chancellor,

THE questions concerning the king's
prerogative and the people's privileges are
nice and difficult. Mr. William Colvin,
who was one of the wifest men this nation ever had, ufed to fay concerning de-
fenfive arms, that he wifhed all princes
thought them lawful, and the people un-
lawful.   And indeed I heartily wifh, that
fomething like thefe moderate fentiments
might always determine all matters in
queftion between both. By the conftitution of this kingdom, no act of the
eftates had the force of a law, unlefs
touched by the king's fceptre, which was
his undoubted prerogative. The touch of
his fceptre gave authority to our laws, as
his

his ſtamp did a currency to our coin : but he had no right to refuſe or with-hold either. It is pretended by ſome men, that, in virtue of this act, the king may refuſe the royal aſſent to acts paſſed by the eſtates of the kingdom. But it ought to be conſidered, that this law is only an acknowledgment and declaration of the king's prerogative, and conſequently gives nothing new to the prince. The act acknowledges this to be the prerogative of the king, that whatever is paſſed in this houſe, cannot have the force of a law without the royal aſſent, and makes it high treaſon to queſtion this prerogative ; becauſe the parliament, during the civil war, had uſurped a power of impoſing their own votes upon the people for law, though neither the king, nor any perſon commiſſionated by him were preſent : and

N

this

this new law was wholly and simply directed to abolish and rescind that usurpa-
tion, as appears by the tenour and express
words of the act; which does neither acknowledge nor declare, that the prince
has a power to refuse the royal assent to
any act presented by the parliament. If
any one should say, that the lawgivers
designed no less, and that the principal
contrivers and promoters of the act frequently boasted they had obtained the
negative, as they call it, for the crown; I
desire to know how they will make that
appear, since no words are to be found in
the act, that shew any such design : especially if we consider that this law was
made by a parliament that spoke the most
plainly, least equivocally, and most fully,
of all others concerning the prerogative.
And if those who promoted the passing of

this

this act were under so strong a delusion, to think they had obtained a new and great prerogative to the crown by a declaratory law, in which there is not one word to that purpose, it was the hand of Heaven that defeated their design of destroying the liberty of their country. I know our princes have refused their assent to some acts since the making of this law: but a practice introduced in arbitrary times can deserve no consideration. For my own part, I am far from pushing things to extremity on either hand: I heartily enter into the sentiments of the wise man I mentioned before, and think the people of this nation might have been happy in mistaking the meaning of this law, if such men, as have had the greatest credit with our princes, would have let them into the true sense of it. And therefore those,

N 2　　　　　　who

who have the honour to advife her majefty, fhould beware of inducing her to a
refufal of the royal affent to the act for
the fecurity of the kingdom, becaufe the
unwarrantable cuftom of rejecting acts
was introduced in arbitrary times.

XII.

MY LORD CHANCELLOR,

IT is often faid in this houfe, that parliaments, and efpecially long feffions of
parliament, are a heavy tax and burden
to this nation: I fuppofe they mean as
things are ufually managed: otherwife I
fhould think it a great reflection on the
wifdom of the nation, and a maxim very
pernicious to our government. But indeed in the prefent ftate of things, they
are a very great burden to us. Our parliament

liament feldom meets in winter, when the
feafon of the year, and our own private
affairs, bring us to town. We are called together for the moſt part in fummer, when
our country buſineſs, and the goodneſs of
the feafon, make us live in town with regret. Our parliaments are ſitting both in
feed time and harveſt, and we are made to
toil the whole year. We meet one day in
three; though no reafon can be given why
we ſhould not meet every day, unlefs fuch
a one as I am unwilling to name, left
thereby occafion ſhould be taken to mention it elfewhere to the reproach of the
nation. The expences of our commif-
ſioners are now become greater than thofe
of our kings formerly were: and a great
part of this money is laid out upon equi-
page, and other things of foreign manufacture, to the great damage of the king-

N 3   dom.

dom. We meet in this place in the after-
noon, after a great dinner, which I think
is not the time of doing bufinefs; and are
in fuch confufion after the candles are
lighted, that very often the debate of one
fingle point cannot be finifhed; but muft
be put off to another day. Parliaments
are forced to fubmit to the conveniences
of the lords of the feffion, and meetings
of the boroughs; though no good reafon
can be given, why either a lord of the
feffion, or any one deputed to the meetings of the boroughs, fhould be a member
of this houfe; but, on the contrary, experience has taught us the inconvenience
of both. When members of parliament,
to perform the duty they owe to their
country, have left the moft important affairs, and quitted their friends many times
in the utmoft extremity, to be prefent at
this

this place, they are told they may return again; as we were the other day called together only in order to be difmiffed. We have been for feveral days adjourned in this time of harveft, when we had the moft important affairs under deliberation; that as well thofe, who have neither place nor penfion, might grow weary of their attendance, as thofe whofe ill ftate of health makes the fervice of their country as dangerous, though no lefs honourable than if they ferved in the field. Do not thefe things fhew us the neceffity of thofe limitations I had the honour to offer to this houfe? and particularly of that for lodging the power of adjournments in the parliament; that for meetings of parliament to be in winter; that for impowering the prefident to give the royal affent, and afcertaining his falary; with that for ex-

cluding

cluding all lords of the feffion from being members of parliament? Could one imagine that in this parliament, in which we have had the firft opportunity of amending our conftitution by new conditions of government, occafion fhould be given by reiterating former abufes, to convince all men of the neceffity of farther limitations upon a fucceffor? Or is not this rather to be attributed to a peculiar providence, that thofe who are the great oppofers of limitations, fhould, by their conduct, give the beft reafon for them? But I hope no member of this houfe will be difcouraged either by delay or oppofition; becaufe the liberties of a people are not to be maintained without paffing through great difficulties, and that no toil and labours ought to be declined to preferve a nation from flavery.

XIII.

XIII.

My Lord Chancellor,

I HAVE waited long and with great patience for the refult of this feffion, to fee if I could difcover a real and fincere intention in the members of this houfe, to reftore the freedom of our country in this great and, perhaps, only opportunity. I know there are many different views among us, and all men pretend the good of the nation. But every man here is obliged carefully to examine the things before us, and to act according to his knowledge and confcience, without regard to the views of other men, whatever charity he may have for them: I fay, every man in this place is obliged, by the

oath

oath he has taken, to give such advice as he thinks most expedient for the good of his country. The principal business of this session has been the forming of an act for the security of the kingdom, upon the expiration of the present entail of the crown. And though one would have thought, that the most essential thing which could have entered into such an act, had been to ascertain the conditions on which the nation would receive a successor, yet this has been entirely waved and over-ruled by the house. Only there is a caution inserted in the act, that the successor shall not be the same person who is to succeed in England, unless such conditions of government be first enacted, as may secure the freedom of this nation, But this is a general and indefinite clause, and liable to the dangerous inconveniency

of

of being declared to be fulfilled by giving us two or three inconfiderable laws. So that this feffion of parliament, in which we have had fo great an opportunity of making ourfelves for ever a free people, is like to terminate without any real fecurity for our liberties, or any effential amendant of our conftitution. And now, when we ought to come to particulars, and enact fuch limitations as may fully fatisfy the general claufe, we muft amufe ourfelves with things of little fignificancy, and hardly mention any limitation of moment or confequence. But inftead of this, acts are brought in for regulations to take place during the life of the queen, which we are not to expect, and quite draw us off from the bufinefs we fhould attend. By thefe methods divers well-meaning men have been deluded, whilft others

have

have propofed a prefent nomination of a fucceffor under limitations. But I fear the far greater part have defigned to make their court either to her majefty, the houfe of Hanover, or thofe of St. Germains, by maintaining the prerogative in Scotland as high as ever, to the perpetual enflaving of this nation to the minifters of England. Therefore I, who have never made court to any prince, and I hope never fhall, at the rate of the leaft prejudice to my country, think myfelf obliged, in difcharge of my confcience, and the duty of my oath in parliament, to offer fuch limitations as may anfwer the general claufe in the act for the fecurity of the kingdom. And this I do in two draughts, the one containing the limitations by themfelves; the other with the fame limitations, and a blank for inferting the name

of

of a fucceffor. If the houfe fhall think fit to take into confideration that draught which has no blank, and enact the limitations, I fhall reft fatisfied, being as little fond of naming a fucceffor as any man. Otherwife, I offer the draught with a blank; to the end that every man may make his court to the perfon he moft affects; and hope by this means to pleafe all parties: the court, in offering them an opportunity to name the fucceffor of England, a thing fo acceptable to her majefty and that nation: thofe who may favour the court of St. Germains, by giving them a chance for their pretenfions; and every true Scotfman, in vindicating the liberty of this nation, whoever be the fucceffor.

FIRST

FIRST DRAUGHT.

'OUR sovereign lady, with advice and
' confent of the eftates of parliament, fta-
' tutes and ordains, that after the deceafe
' of her majefty, whom God long pre-
' ferve, and failing heirs of her body, no
' one fhall fucceed to the crown of this
' realm that is likewife fucceffor to the
' crown of England, but under the limi-
' tations following, which, together with
' the oath of coronation and claim of
' right, they fhall fwear to obferve. That
' all places and offices, both civil and mili-
' tary, and all penfions formerly conferred
' by our kings, fhall ever after be given
' by parliament.—That a new parliament
' fhall be chofen every Michaelmas head-
' court,

' court, to fit the firſt of November there-
' after, and adjourn themſelves from time
' to time till next Michaelmas; and that
' they chooſe their own preſident.——That a
' committee of thirty-ſix members, choſen
' by and out of the whole parliament,
' without diſtinction of eſtates, ſhall, dur-
' ing the intervals of parliament, under the
' king, have the adminiſtration of the
' government, be his council, and account-
' able to parliament; with power, in ex-
' traordinary occaſions, to call the parlia-
' ment together.'

SECOND DRAUGHT.

' OUR ſovereign lady, with advice and
' conſent of the eſtates of parliament, ſta-
' tutes and ordains, that after the deceaſe
' of

' of her majesty, whom God long pre-
' serve, and heirs of her body failing,   .
'   shall succeed to the
' crown of this realm. But that in case
' the said successor be likewise the suc-
' cessor to the crown of England, the
' said successor shall be under the limita-
' tions following,' &c.

No man can be an enemy to these limitations, in case we have the same king
with England, except he who is so shame-
less a partisan either of the court at St.
Germains, or the house of Hanover, that
he would rather see Scotland continue to
depend upon an English ministry, than
that their prerogative should be any way
lessened in this kingdom. As for those
who have St. Germains in their view, and
are accounted the highest of all the pre-
                                    rogative-

rogative-men, I would aſk them, if we ſhould aſſiſt them in advancing their prince to the throne of Great Britain, are we, for our reward, to continue ſtill in our former dependence on the Engliſh court? Theſe limitations are the only teſt to diſcover a lover of his country from a courtier either to her majeſty, Hanover, or St. Germains. For prerogative men, who are for enſlaving this nation to the directions of another court, are courtiers to any ſucceſſor; and let them pretend what they will, if their principles lead neceſſarily to ſubject this nation to another, are enemies to the nation. Theſe men are ſo abſurd as to pro-voke England, and yet reſolve to continue ſlaves of that court. This country muſt be made a field of blood, in order to advance a papiſt to the throne of Britain. If we fail, we ſhall be ſlaves by right of

O

conqueſt;

conqueſt; if we prevail, have the happi-
neſs to continue in our former ſlaviſh dependence. And though to break this yoke,
all good men would venture their all, yet
I believe few will be willing to lie at the
mercy of France and popery, and at the
ſame time draw upon themſelves the indignation and power of England, for the
ſake only of meaſuring our ſtrength with
a much more powerful nation; and to be
ſure to continue ſtill under our former dependence, though we ſhould happen to
prevail. Now, of thoſe who are for the
ſame ſucceſſor with England, I would aſk,
if in that caſe we are not alſo to continue
in our former dependence; which will not
fail always to grow from bad to worſe,
and at length become more intolerable to
all honeſt men, than death itſelf. For my
own part, I think, that even the moſt

zealous

zealous proteſtant in the nation, if he have a true regard for his country, ought rather to wiſh, were it conſiſtent with our claim of right, that a papiſt ſhould ſucceed to the throne of Great Britain, under ſuch limitations as would render this nation free and independent, than the moſt proteſtant and beſt prince, without any. If we may live free, I little value who is king: it is indifferent to me, provided the limitations be enacted, to name or not name; Hanover, St Germains, or whom you will.

XIV.

MY LORD CHANCELLOR,

HIS grace, the high commiſſioner, having acquainted this houſe, that he has inſtructions from her majeſty, to give the

O 2

royal

royal affent to all acts paffed in this feffion,
except that for the fecurity of the kingdom, it will be highly neceffary to provide fome new laws for fecuring our
liberty upon the expiration of the prefent
entail of the crown. And therefore I fhall
fpeak to the firft article of the limitations
contained in the fhort act I offered the
other day; not only becaufe it is the firft
in order, but becaufe I perfuade myfelf
you all know that parliaments were formerly chofen annually; that they had the
power of appointing the times of their
meetings and adjournments, together with
the nomination of committees to fuper-
intend the adminiftration of the government during the intervals of parliament:
all which, if it were neceffary, might be
proved by a great number of public acts.
So that if I demonftrate the ufe and ne-

ceffity

ceffity of the firft article, there will remain no great difficulty concerning the reft.

My Lord Chancellor,

THE condition of a people, however unhappy, if they not only know the caufe of their mifery, but have alfo the remedy in their power, and yet fhould refufe to apply it, one would think, were not to be pitied. And though the condition of good men, who are concluded and oppreffed by a majority of the bad, is much to be lamented; yet chriftianity teaches us to fhew a greater meafure of compaffion to thofe who are knowingly and voluntarily obftinate to ruin both themfelves and others. But the regret of every wife and good man muft needs be extraordinary, when he fees the liberty and happinefs of his

O 3   country

country not only obftructed, but utterly
extinguifhed by the private and tranfitory
intereft of felf-defigning men, who indeed
very often meet their own ruin, but moft
certainly bring deftruction upon their pof-
terity by fuch courfes. Sure, if a man who
is intrufted by others, fhould, for his own
private advantage, betray that truft, to the
perpetual and irrecoverable ruin of thofe
who trufted him, the livelieft fenfe and
deepeft remorfe for fo great guilt, will undoubtedly feize and terrify the confcience
of fuch a man, as often as the treacherous
part he has acted fhall recur to his
thoughts; which will moft frequently
happen in the times of his diftrefs, and
the nearer he approaches to a life in
which thofe remorfes are perpetual. But
I hope every man in this houfe has fo
well confidered thefe things, as to preferve

him

him from falling into such terrible circumstances: and (as all men are subject
to great failings) if any person, placed in
this most eminent trust, is conscious to
himself of having ever been wanting in
duty to his country, I doubt not he will
this day, in this weighty matter, atone for
all, and not blindly follow the opinion
of other men, because he alone must account for his own actions to his grea
Lord and Master.

The limitation, to which I am about
to speak, requires, that all places, offices,
and pensions, which have been formerly
given by our kings, shall, after her majesty
and heirs of her body, be conferred by
parliament, so long as we are under the
same prince with England. Without this
limitation, our poverty and subjection to
the court of England will every day in-

          crease;

creaſe; and the queſtion we have now before us is, whether we will be freemen or
ſlaves for ever? whether we will continue
to depend, or break the yoke of our dependence? and whether we will chooſe to
live poor and miſerable, or rich, free, and
happy? Let no man think to object, that
this limitation takes away the whole power
of the prince.   For the ſame condition of
government is found in one of the moſt
abſolute monarchies of the world.   I have
very good authority for what I ſay, from
all the beſt authors that have treated of the
government of China; but ſhall only cite
the words of an able miniſter of ſtate,
who had very well conſidered whatever
had been written on that ſubject; I mean
Sir William Temple, who ſays, ‘ That for
‘ the government, it is abſolute monarchy,
‘ there being no other laws in China,
                                        ‘ but

' but the king's orders and commands;
' and it is likewife hereditary, ftill de-
' fcending to the next of blood.   But all
' orders and commands of the king pro-
' ceed through his councils; and are made
' upon the recommendation or petition of
' the council proper and appointed for that
' affair: fo that all matters are debated, de-
' termined, and concluded by the feveral
' councils; and then upon their advices
' and requefts made to the king, they are
' ratified and figned by him, and fo pafs
' into laws.   All great offices of ftate are
' likewife conferred by the king, upon the
' fame recommendations or petitions of
' his feveral councils; fo that none are
' preferred by the humour of the prince
' himfelf, nor by favour of any minifter,
' by flattery or corruption, but by the
' force or appearance of merit, of learn-
' ing,

' ing, and of virtue; which obferved by
' the feveral councils, gain their recom-
' mendations or petitions to the king.'
Thefe are the exprefs words of that minifter. And if under the greateft abfolute
monarchy of the world, in a country
where the prince actually refides; if among
heathens this be accounted a neceffary part
of government for the encouragement of
virtue, fhall it be denied to Chriftians living under a prince who refides in another
nation ? Shall it be denied to a people,
who have a right to liberty, and yet are
not capable of any in their prefent circum-
ftances without this limitation ? But we
have formed to ourfelves fuch extravagant notions of government, that even in
a limited monarchy nothing will pleafe,
which in the leaft deviates from the model
of France, and every thing elfe muft ftand

3

branded

branded with the name of commonwealth. Yet a great and wife people found this very condition of government neceffary to fupport even an abfolute monarchy. If any man fay, that the empire of China contains divers kingdoms; and that the care of the emperor, and his knowledge of particular men, cannot extend to all: I anfwer, the cafe is the fame with us; and it feems as if that wife people defigned this conftitution for a remedy to the like inconveniences with thofe we labour under at this time.

This limitation will undoubtedly enrich the nation, by ftopping that perpetual iffue of money to England, which has reduced this country to extreme poverty. This limitation does not flatter us with the hopes of riches by an uncertain project; does not require fo much as the condition

dition of our own induftry; but, by faving great fums to the country, will every year furnifh a ftock fufficient to carry on a confiderable trade, or to eftablifh fome ufeful manufacture at home, with the higheft probability of fuccefs: becaufe our minifters, by this rule of government, would be freed from the influence of Eng-lifh councils; and our trade be entirely in our own hands, and not under the power of the court, as it was in the affair of Da-rien. If we do not obtain this limitation, our attendance at London will continue to drain this nation of all thofe fums which fhould be a ftock for trade. Be-fides, by frequenting that court, we not only fpend our money, but learn the ex-penfive modes and ways of living, of a rich and luxurious nation: we lay out yearly great fums in furniture and equi-

page,

page, to the unfpeakable prejudice of the trade and manufactures of our own country. Not that I think it amifs to travel into England, in order to fee and learn their induftry in trade and hufbandry. But at court what can we learn, except a horrid corruption of manners, and an expenfive way of living, that we may for ever after be both poor and profligate?

This limitation will fecure to us our freedom and independence. It has been often faid in this houfe, that our princes are captives in England; and inded one would not wonder if, when our intereft happens to be different from that of England, our kings, who muft be fupported by the riches and power of that nation in all their undertakings, fhould prefer an Englifh intereft before that of this country. It is yet lefs ftrange, that

Englifh

English ministers should advise and procure the advancement of such persons to
the ministry of Scotland, as will comply
with their measures and the king's orders;
and to surmount the difficulties they may
meet with from a true Scots interest,
that places and pensions should be be-
stowed upon parliament-men and others:
I say, these things are so far from wonder,
that they are inevitable in the present
state of our affairs. But I hope they
likewise shew us, that we ought not to
continue any longer in this condition.
Now, this limitation is advantageous to
all. The prince will no more be put
upon the hardship of deciding between
an English and a Scots interest; or the
difficulty of reconciling what he owes
to each nation, in consequence of his
coronation oath. Even English ministers

will

will no longer lie under the temptation of meddling in Scots affairs: nor the minifters of this kingdom, together with all thofe who have places and penfions, be any more fubject to the worft of all flavery. But if the influences I mentioned before fhall ftill continue, what will any other limitation avail us? What fhall we be the better for our act concerning the power of war and peace? fince, by the force of an Englifh intereft and influence, we cannot fail of being engaged in every war, and neglected in every peace.

By this limitation, our parliament will become the moft uncorrupted fenate of all Europe. No man will be tempted to vote againft the intereft of his country, when his country fhall have all the bribes in her own hands; offices, places, penfions. It
will

will be no longer neceffary to lofe one
half of the public cuftoms, that parliament-men may be made collectors. We
will not defire to exclude the officers of
ftate from fitting in this houfe, when the
country fhall have the nomination of them;
and our parliaments, free from corruption,
cannot fail to redrefs all our grievances.
We fhall then have no caufe to fear a refufal of the royal affent 'to our acts; for
we fhall have no evil counfellor, nor
enemy of his country, to advife it.   When
this condition of government fhall take
place, the royal affent will be the ornament of the prince, and never be refufed
to the defires of the people.   A general
unanimity will be found in this houfe,
in every part of the government, and
among all ranks and conditions of men.
The distinctions of court and country

party shall no more be heard in this nation; nor shall the prince and people
any longer have a different interest. Rewards and punishments will be in the
hands of those who live among us, and
consequently best know the merit of men;
by which means, virtue will be recom-
penfed, and vice difcouraged, and the
reign and government of the prince will
flourish in peace and juftice.

I should never make an end, if I should
profecute all the great advantages of this
limitation; which, like a divine influence,
turns all to good, as the want of it has
hitherto poifoned every thing, and brought
all to ruin. I shall therefore only add
one particular more, in which it will be
of the higheft advantage to this nation.
We all know, that the only way of enflaving a people is by keeping up a ftand-

P   ing

ing army; that by standing forces all
limited monarchies have been deftroyed;
without them none; that fo long as any
ftanding forces are allowed in a nation,
pretexts will never be wanting to increafe
them; that princes have never fuffered
militias to be put upon any good foot,
left ftanding forces fhould appear unneceffary. We alfo know that a good and
well-regulated militia is of fo great im-,
portance to a nation, as to be the principal
part of the conftitution of any free government. Now, by this limitation, the nation will have a fufficient power to render
their militia good and effectual, by the
nomination of officers: and if we would
fend a certain proportion of our militia
abroad yearly, and relieve them from time
to time, we may make them as good as
thofe of Switzerland are; and much more

able

able to defend the country, than any
unactive ftanding forces can be. We
may fave every year great fums of money,
which are now expended to maintain a
ftanding army, and, which is yet more,
run no hazard of lofing our liberty by
them. We may employ a greater number
of officers in thofe detachments, than we
do at prefent in all our forces both at
home and abroad; and make better conditions for them in thofe countries that
need their affiftance. For being freed
from the influences of Englifh councils,
we fhall certainly look better than we
have hitherto done to the terms on which
we may fend them into the armies either
of England or Holland; and not permit
them to be abufed fo many different ways,
as, to the great reproach of the nation,
they have been, in their rank, pay, cloth-

ing, arrears, levy-money, quarters, tranf-
port-fhips, and gratuities.

Having thus fhewn fome of the great
advantages this limitation will bring to
the nation (to which every one of you
will be able to add many more); that it
is not only confiftent with monarchy,
but even with an abfolute monarchy:
having demonftrated the neceffity of fuch
a condition in all empires, which contain
feveral kingdoms; and that without it
we muft for ever continue in a dependence upon the court of England; in the
name of God, what hinders us from em-
bracing fo great a bleffing? Is it becaufe
her majefty will refufe the royal affent
to this act? If fhe do, fure I am, fuch a
refufal muft proceed from the advice of
Englifh counfellors; and will not that
be a demonftration to us, that after her
majefty,

majesty, and heirs of her body, we must not, cannot any longer continue under the same prince with England? Shall we be wanting to ourselves? Can her majesty give her assent to this limitation upon a successor before you offer it to her? Is she at liberty to give us satisfaction in this point, till we have declared to England, by a vote of this house, that unless we obtain this condition, we will not name the successor with them? And then will not her majesty, even by English advice, be persuaded to give her assent; unless her counsellors shall think fit to incur the heavy imputation, and run the dangerous risk, of dividing these nations for ever? If therefore either reason, honour, or conscience, have any influence upon us; if we have any regard either to ourselves or posterity; if there be any

such

such thing as virtue, happiness, or reputation in this world, or felicity in a future state, let me adjure you by all these not to draw upon your heads everlasting infamy, attended with the eternal reproaches and anguish of an evil conscience, by making yourselves and your posterity miserable.

E S S A Y

ON THE

GENIUS, CHARACTER, AND WRITINGS

OF

JAMES THOMSON

THE POET.

Intended as a Baſis for writing properly the Life of
that truly excellent Man.

By DAVID STUART, EARL OF BUCHAN.

To the Shade of Thomſon.

If Britain, palſied, cannot feel theſe lays
Warm in the heart, and burſting forth thy praiſe,
Me from Bœotia let the fates convey,
Or death remove me to a brighter day;
To ſcenes exalted, where the noble ſouls
Of men like thee no ſervile court controuls;
Scenes where the good no modeſt worth conceals,
And where no praiſe the worthleſs coxcomb ſteals!

E S S A Y, &c.

POETRY, that divine energy (for I cannot call it art) which lifts the man of clay from the dirty world he inhabits to the regions of fancy, is a gift of Heaven, and, like all her gifts, is inimitable, and difficult to be defcribed.

In the philofophical, or as I would rather choofe to call it, original language of the Greeks, it is expreffed by a vocable defcriptive of its power, which is creation.

In the Gothic, and all its derivatives in all languages approaching to originality, the name is fynonymous. In old Englifh

and

and Scottish it is called *making*, and poets were denominated makers.

It is my purpose in the following Essay to honour and describe the chief maker of Scotland; to shew the superiority of his genius, to do justice to his character as a man, and to illustrate his merit as an author, by exhibiting examples of them all.

I shall begin with a quotation from Samuel Johnson's Preface to Thomson's Poems, because it is well expressed, and will furnish a good text for illustrating the genius of the poet; though it is evident from Johnson's verses, that he himself was very far from being a maker.

In the counterpoint (as I may call it) of poetry he was a master; but of the grounds and melodies he was incapable.

What

What then is *taste,* but the internal powers
Active, and strong, and feelingly alive
To each fine impulfe ? a difcerning fenfe
Of decent and fublime, with quick difguft
From things deform'd, or difarranged, or grofs
In fpecies ? This, nor gems, nor ftores of gold,
Nor purple ftate, *nor culture* can beftow;
But God alone, when firft his active hand
Imprints the fecret bias of the foul.

Pleafures of the Imag. b. iii. v. 515.

" Thomfon's mode of thinking and of expreffing his thoughts (writes Johnfon) is original. His blank verfe is no more the blank verfe of Milton, or of any other poet, than the rhymes of Prior are the rhymes of Cowley. His numbers, his paufes, his diction, are of his own growth, without tranfcription, without imitation. He thinks in a peculiar train, and he thinks always as a man of genius; he looks round on nature and on life with the eye which na-

3ture

ture beſtows only on a poet; the eye that diſtinguiſhes, in every thing preſented to its view, whatever there is on which imagination can delight to be detained, and with a mind that at once comprehends the vaſt, and attends to the minute.

" The reader of the Seaſons wonders that he never ſaw before what Thomſon ſhews him, and that he never yet has felt what Thomſon impreſſes."

It was emphatically ſaid by the greateſt of men to his audience, when he was explaining the vital principles of holineſs, " He that hath ears to hear, let him hear!" So it is needleſs to muſter up a legion of words to infuſe the knowledge of what conſtitutes a genuine poet. The genius of a poet will bear witneſs to itſelf. Poetry is the flower of ſentiment, and muſic is its odour; ſo that what is ſaid of the one is proportionably applicable to the other;

other; and Rousseau's description of genius in music will be found equally just in the one as in the other. " Seek not to know what is genius; if thou hast it, thy feelings will tell thee what it is; if thou hast it not, thou never wilt know it."—&c.

Yet as the chaste enjoyment of beauty, and the just perception of the symmetry and picturesque perfection of nature, is in the highest degree conducive to the sense and practice of virtue, it is of high moment to enquire what kind of culture is most friendly to the attainment of taste, which is the handmaid of genius.

May it not be rationally supposed, that, without any predisposing circumstances in the bodily frame, a child will receive the impressions that are most conducive to that glorious combination of them

6   (which,

(which, when matured to permanent thought, we call genius) in the country, more readily than in towns or villages, where every thing is too complex for their underftanding?

Will not an education lefs artificial, and tending more to fpontaneous contemplation of natural objects, be more favourable to its attainment than the contrary? And would it not be proper to allow children to feed more upon their own thoughts than on the thoughts and inftructions of others?

Would it not be better to have lefs myftery and technical inftitution in infancy and youth, and more natural knowledge and fentiment than we fee exhibited in fchools and private tuition? And laftly, would it not be better to beftow more time in forming philofophers and citizens,

than

than in training up schoolmasters and milliners?—But here I stop. Thomson passed his infancy and early youth in the picturesque and pastoral country of Tiviotdale in Scotland, which is full of the elements of natural beauty, wood, water, eminence and rock, with intermixture of rich and beautiful meadow. The horison was bounded by the Cheviot, a land of song and of heroic achievement; the venerable ruins of Jedburgh, Dryburgh, Kelso, and Melrose, were at hand, to add suitable impressions to the whole.

His mother had been well educated, was a woman of uncommon sensibility, and endowed with sublime affections.

He was cherished by Sir William Bennet, at Chesters, near Jedburgh, the most accomplished country gentleman in that part of Scotland. Every thing un-

doubtedly

doubtedly confpired to attune the genius
of Thomfon to fentiment and fong.

" He afk'd no more than fimple nature gave,
" He lov'd the mountains, and enjoy'd their ftorms;
" No falfe defires, no pride-created wants
" Difturb'd the peaceful current of his time,
" And through the reftlefs, ever-tortur'd maze
" Of pleafure or ambition, bid it rage."

It is believed that, at Dryburgh, with
Mr. Haliburton, of New-mains, a friend
of his father's, he firft tuned his Doric
reed, to which he alludes in his Autumn:

" Wafh'd lovely from the Tweed (pure parent ftream),
" Whofe paftoral banks firft heard my Doric reed.

Sir Gilbert Elliot of Minto (too), afterwards Lord Juftice Clerk, a man of elegant tafte, was kind to young Thomfon.

Thomfon fent him a copy of the firft
edition of his Seafons, which Sir Gilbert

fhewing

shewing to a relation of the poet's who was gardener at Minto, he took the book, which was finely bound, into his hands, and having turned it round and round, and gazed on it for some time, Sir Gilbert said to him, " Well, David, what do you think of James Thomson now? There's a book that will make him famous all over the world, and his name immortal!" " Indeed, Sir," said David, " that is a grand book! I did not think the lad had had ingenuity enough to have done such a neat piece of handicraft."

Striking example of the effects of situation and culture upon taste and sentiment!

That 'Thomson's youth was respectable appears from the countenance he

Q   received

received from Meffrs. Riccalton and Gufthart ; and the continued attentions of the
latter to the children of Mrs. Thomfon
reflect honour upon his memory, and
excite fentiments in the feeling heart
that deferve to be meditated and revolved:
and I hope I am not writing for Chinefe
pedlars, with fteel-yards at their button-
holes, but to men and women who have
ftill fomething in them that preceded the
corruption of our commonwealth!

Thomfon, having been encouraged by
Lady Grizel Baillie to try his fortunes
in London, embarked at Leith in the
autumn of the year 1725, bedewed with
the tears of his amiable and affectionate
mother, the heart-felt recollection of which
produced on her death, which happened not
long after, the following unpremeditated

but

but beautiful verſes, which, though not prepared for the preſs, I have given from a copy in the author's own hand-writing.

ON THE DEATH OF HIS MOTHER *.

From an original, in the Poet's own hand-writing, in the collection of the Earl of Buchan.

YE fabled muſes, I your aid diſclaim,
Your airy raptures, and your fancied flame:
True genuine woe my throbbing breaſt inſpires,
Love prompts my lays, and filial duty fires;
The ſoul ſprings inſtant at the warm deſign,
And the heart dictates every flowing line.
See! where the kindeſt, beſt of mothers lies,
And death has ſhut her ever-weeping eyes;
Has lodg'd at laſt peace in her weary breaſt,
And lull'd her many piercing cares to reſt.
No more the orphan train around her ſtands,
While her full heart upbraids her needy hands!

---

* Elizabeth Trotter, of a genteel family in the neighbourhood of Greenlaw in Berwickſhire.

No more the widow's lonely fate fhe feels,

The fhock fevere that modeft want conceals,

Th' oppreffor's fcourge, the fcorn of wealthy pride,

And poverty's unnumber'd ills befide.

For fee ! attended by th' angelic throng,

Through yonder worlds of light fhe glides along,

And claims the well earn'd raptures of the fky.—

Yet fond concern recalls the mother's eye ;

She feeks the helplefs orphans left behind ;

So hardly left ! fo bitterly refign'd !

Still, ftill ! is fhe my foul's divineft theme,

The waking vifion, and the wailing dream :

Amid the ruddy fun's enliv'ning blaze

O'er my dark eyes her dewy image plays,

And in the dread dominion of the night

Shines out again the fadly pleafing fight.

Triumphant virtue all around her darts,

And more than volumes ev'ry look imparts—

Looks, foft, yet awful, melting, yet ferene,

Where both the mother and the faint are feen.

But ah ! that night—that torturing night remains;

May darknefs dye it with its deepeft ftains,

May joy on it forfake her rofy bow'rs,

And fcreaming forrow blaft its baleful hours,

When

When on the margin of the briny flood *
Chill'd with a sad presaging damp I stood,
Took the last look, ne'er to behold her more,
And mix'd our murmurs with the wavy roar,
Heard the last words fall from her pious tongue,
Then, wild into the bulging vessel flung,
Which soon, too soon convey'd me from *her* sight
Dearer than life, and liberty and light!
Why was I then, ye powers, reserv'd for this?
Nor sunk that moment in the vast abyss?
Devour'd at once by the relentless wave,
And whelm'd for ever in a wat'ry grave?—
Down, ye wild wishes of unruly woe!—
I see her with immortal beauty glow,
The early wrinkle care-contracted gone,
Her tears all wiped, and all her sorrows flown;
Th' exalting voice of Heav'n I hear her breathe,
To sooth her soul in agonies of death.
I see her through the mansions blest above,
And now she meets her dear expecting love.
Heart-cheering sight! but yet, alas! o'erspread
By the damp gloom of Grief's uncheerful shade,

---

* On the shore of Leith, when he embarked for
London.

Q 3

Come

Come then of reafon the reflecting hour,
And let me truft the kind o'er-ruling Power,
Who from the right commands the fhining day,
The poor man's portion, and the orphan's ftay !

THOMSON'S ELEGY ON THE DEATH OF AIKMAN, THE
PAINTER *.

*From a MS. of the Author's own hand-writing in the
collection of the Earl of Buchan.*

OH could I draw, my friend, thy genuine mind,
Juft, as the living forms by thee defign'd,
Of Raphael's figures none fhould fairer fhine,
Nor Titian's colours longer laft than mine.

A mind

---

* Mr. Aikman died at London, on the 7th of June,
O. S. 1731, from whence his remains were fent to Scotland,
and interred in the Gray-Friars church-yard, clofe by
thofe of his only fon, who had been buried only a few
months before.

Mr. Aikman was the fon of William Aikman of Cairny,
Efq. (fheriff depute of Forfarfhire, a lawyer of eminence,

and

A mind in wifdom old, in lenience young,

From fervent truth where every virtue fprung;

Where all was real, modeft, plain, fincere;

Worth above fhow, and goodnefs unfevere:

View'd round and round, as lucid diamonds throw

Still as you turn them a revolving glow;

So did his mind reflect with fecret ray,

In various virtues, heav'n's internal day,

Whether in high difcourfe it foar'd fublime,

And fprung impatient o'er the bounds of Time,

---

and in nomination for a judge's gown at the time of his death) by Margaret, fifter of Sir John Clerk of Pennycuik, Baronet.

He was born on the 24th of October 1682, and was educated by his parents with great care, and deftined for the profeffion of the law. Nature thought fit to deftine and fit him for another more elegant, not lefs liberal, and certainly much more delightful. He went to Italy in the year 1705, and returned to Britain in 1710, not only a good painter, but an accomplifhed and agreeable man.

In the Gothic reigns of George I. and II. he could look for nothing but money for ftarch heads and periwigs, and ftarch heads and periwigs was he forced to delineate and paint till his dying day. O che fciagura!

Q 4

Or

Or wand'ring nature through with raptur'd eye,
Ador'd the hand that turn'd yon azure fky:
Whether to focial life he bent his thought,
And the right poife of mingling paffions fought,
Gay converfe blefs'd; or in the thoughtful grove
Bid the heart open every fource of love.
New varying lights ftill fet before your eyes
The juft, the good, the focial, or the wife.
For fuch a death who can, who would, refufe
The friend a tear, a verfe the mournful mufe?
Yet pay we juft acknowledgment to Heaven,
Though fnatch'd fo foon, that Aikman e'er was
  given.

A friend, when dead, is but remov'd from fight,
Hid in the luftre of eternal light:
Oft with the mind he wonted converfe keeps
In the lone walk, or when the body fleeps
Lets in a wand'ring ray, and all elate
Wings and attracts her to another ftate;*
And when the parting ftorms of life are o'er,
May yet rejoin him on a happier fhore.

---

* This and the three preceding lines are not in the
MS. of Mrs. Forbes Aikman.

As

As thofe we love decay, we die in part,

String after ftring is fever'd from the heart;

Till loofen'd life at laft—but breathing clay,

Without one pang, is glad to fall away.

Unhappy he who lateft feels the blow,

Whofe eyes have wept o'er ev'ry friend laid low,

Dragg'd ling'ring on from partial death to death,

And dying, all he can refign is breath.

Song written in his early Years, and afterwards shaped for his Amanda.

From a MS. in the collection of the Earl of Buchan.

FOR ever, Fortune, wilt thou prove

An unrelenting foe to love;

And when we meet a mutual heart,

Come in between and bid us part;

Bid us figh on from day to day,

And wifh and wifh the foul away;

Till youth and genial years are flown,

And all the life of life is gone?

But bufy bufy ftill art thou,

To bind the lovelefs joylefs vow,

The

The heart from pleafure to delude,

And join the gentle to the rude * ;

For pomp, and noife, and fenfelefs fhow,

To make us nature's joys forego,

Beneath a gay dominion groan,

And put the golden fetter on !

To Dr. De la Cour, in Ireland.

On his Profpect of Poetry.

HAIL gently-warbling De la Cour, whofe fame,

Spurning Hibernia's folitary coaft,

Where fmall rewards attend the tuneful throng,

Pervades Britannia's well-difcerning ifle :

In fpite of all the gloomy-minded tribe

That would eclipfe thy fame, ftill fhall the mufe,

High foaring o'er the tall Parnaffian mount

---

* For once, O Fortune ! hear my prayer,

And I abfolve thy future care :

All other bleffings I refign,

Make but the dear Amanda mine !

The original of this alfo, as prepared for his miftrefs,

't in Lord Buchan's poffeffion.

With

With fpreading pinions—fing thy wondrous praife,
In ftrains attun'd to the feraphic lyre.
Sing unappall'd, though mighty be the theme!
O! could fhe in thy own harmonious ftrain,
Where fofteft numbers fmoothly flowing glide
In trickling cadence; where the milky maze
Devolves in filence; by the harfher found
Of hoarfer periods ftill unruffled, could
Her lines but like thine own Euphrates flow—
Then might fhe fing in numbers worthy thee.
But what can language do, when Fancy finds
Herfelf unequal to the lovely tafk?
Can feeble words thy vivid colours paint,
Or fhew the fweets which inexhauftive flow?
Hearken ye woods, and long-refounding groves;
Liften ye ftreams, foft purling thro' the meads,
And hymning horrid, all ye tempefts roar.
Awake, ye woodlands! fing, ye warbling larks,
In wildly lufcious notes! But moft of all,
Attend, ye grateful fair, attend the youth
Who fweetly fings of nature and of you:
From you alone his confcious breaft expects
Its foft rewards, by fordid love of gain
Unbiafs'd, undebas'd; to meaner minds

Belong

Belong fuch narrow views; his nobler foul,

Tranfported with a gen'rous thirft of fame,

Sublimely rifes with expanded wings,

And through the lucid empyrean foars.

So the young eagle wings its rapid way

Thro' heaven's broad azure; fometimes fprings aloft,

Now drops, now cleaves with even-waving wings

The yielding air, nor feas nor mountains ftop

Its flight impetuous, gazing at the fun

With irretorted eye, whilft he pervades

A tracklefs void, and unexplor'd before.

Long had the curious traveller ftrove to find

The ruins of afpiring Babylon—

In vain—for nought the niceft eye could trace

Save one wide, wat'ry, undiftinguifh'd wafte:

But you with more than magic art have rais'd

Semiramis's city from its grave;

You have revers'd the fcripture curfe, which faid,

Dragons fhall here inhabit; in your page

We view the rifing fpires; the hurried eye

Diftracted wanders through the verdant maze;

In middle air the pendent gardens hang,

Tremendous ceiling!—whilft no folar beam

Falls on the lengthen'd gloom beneath; the woods

Project

Projeſt above a ſteep-alluring ſhade;
The finiſh'd garden opens to the view
Wide-ſtretching viſtas, while the whiſp'ring wind
Dimples along the breezy-ruffled lake.

Now every tree irregular, and buſts
Are prodigal of harmony: the birds
Frequent th' aërial wood, and nature bluſhes,
Aſham'd to find herſelf outdone by art:
Theſe and a thouſand beauties could I ſing,
Collecting like the ever-toiling bee
From yonder mingled wildernefs of flow'rs
The aromatic ſweets; while you, great youth!
O'er thy decaying country chief preſide;
Be thou her genius call'd, inſpire her youth
With noble emulation to arrive
At Helicon's fair font, which few, alas!
Save you, have taſted of Hibernian youth.

Thy country, tho' corrupted, brought thee forth,
And deem'd her greateſt ornament; and now
Regards thee as her brighteſt northern ſtar.
Long may you reign as ſuch; and ſhould grim Time,
With iron teeth, deprive us of our Pope,
Then we'll tranſplant thy blooming laurels freſh
From your bleak ſhore to Albion's happier coaſt.

Thomſon's

*Thomson's Letter to Mr. George Ross *.*

London, November 6th, 1736.

DEAR ROSS,

I OWN I have a good deal of assurance, after asking one favour of you, never to answer your letter till I ask another. But not to mince the matter, and all apologies apart, hearken to my request—My sisters have been advised by their friends to set up at Edinburgh a little milliner's shop; and if you can conveniently advance to them twelve pounds, on my account, it will be a particular favour. That will set them a-going, and I design from time to time to send them goods from hence. My whole account I will pay you when you come up here, not in poetical paper

* From an original in Lord Buchan's collection.

credit,

credit, but in the folid money of this dirty world. I will not draw upon you, in cafe you be not prepared to defend your-felf; but if your purfe be valiant, pleafe to enquire for Jean or Elizabeth Thomfon, at the Reverend Mr. Gufthart's; and if this letter be not a fufficient teftimony of the debt, I will fend you whatever you defire.

It is late, and I would not lofe this poft. Like a laconic man of bufinefs, therefore, I muft here ftop fhort; though I have feveral things to impart to you, and, through your canal, to the deareft, trueft, heartieft youth that treads on Scottifh ground. The next letter I write you fhall be wafhed clean from bufinefs in the Caftalian fountain.

I am whipping and fpurring to finifh a tragedy for you this winter, but am ftill at fome diftance from the goal, which makes me fear being diftanced. Remember me to all friends, and above them all to Mr. Forbes. Though my affection to him is not fanned by letters, yet is it as high as when I was his brother in the virtù, and played at chefs with him in a poft-chaife.

I am, dear Rofs,

Moft fincerely and affectionately yours,

JAMES THOMSON.

Thomfon to Mr. George Rofs.

London, Jan. 12, 1737.

DEAR SIR,

HAVING been entirely in the country of late, finifhing my play, I did not receive yours till fome days ago. It was kind in you not *to draw* rafhly upon me, which at prefent had put me into danger:

but

but very foon (that is to fay, about two months hence) I fhall have a golden buckler, and you may draw boldly.—— My play * is received in Drury-lane play-houfe, and will be put into my lord chamberlain's or his deputy's hands to-morrow.——May we hope to fee you this winter, and to have the affiftance of your hands, in cafe it is acted? What will become of you? I am afraid the *creepy* † and you will be acquainted.——Forbes, I hope, is cheerful, and in good health. Shall we never fee him? or fhall I go to him before he comes to us? I long to fee him, in order to play out that game of chefs which we left unfiniiied. Remember me kindly to him, with all the

* Agamemnon.

† Stool, ufed in the Scotch churches for doing penance.

Rzealous

zealous truth of old friendſhip.   Pettie [*]
came here two or three days ago : I have
not yet ſeen the round man of God to
be.   He is to be parſonified a few days
hence.—How a gown and caſſock will
become him ! and with what a holy leer
he will edify the devout females ! There
is no doubt of his having a call ; for he
is immediately to enter upon a tolerable
living.   God grant him more, and as
fat as himſelf.   It rejoices me to ſee one
worthy, honeſt, excellent man raiſed, at
leaſt to an independency.   Pray make

[*] Rev. Mr. Patrick Murdoch, the oily man of
God of the Caſtle of Indolence.

   " A little, round, fat, oily man of God,
   " Was one I chiefly mark'd among the fry;
   " He had a roguiſh twinkle in his eye,
   " And ſhone all glittering with unholy dew,
   " If a tight damſel chaunc'd to trippen by."

my compliments to my Lord Prefident *
and all friends.   I fhall be glad to hear
more at large from you.   Juft now I
am with the alderman, who wifhes you
all happinefs, and defires his fervice to
Jock.   Believe me to be

Ever moft affectionately yours,
JAMES THOMSON.

*Thomfon to Mr. Lyttelton, afterwards
Lord Lyttelton.*

London, July 14th, 1743.
Dear Sir,

I HAD the pleafure of yours fome
pofts ago, and have delayed anfwering it
hitherto, that I might be able to determine when I could have the happinefs of
waiting upon you.

Hagley is the place in England I moft
defire to fee; I imagine it to be greatly

* Prefident Forbes.

R 2   delightful

delightful in itfelf, and I know it to be fo to the higheft degree by the company it is animated with.

Some reafons prevent my waiting upon you immediately; but if you will be fo good as let me know how long you defign to ftay in the country, nothing fhall hinder me from paffing three weeks or a month with you before you leave it. As this will fall in autumn, I fhall like it the better, for I think that feafon of the year the moft pleafing, and the moft poetical. The fpirits are not then diffipated with the gaiety of fpring, and the glaring light of fummer, but compofed into a ferious and tempered joy.——The year is perfect. In the mean time I will go on with correcting the Seafons, and hope to carry down more than one of them with me. The mufes, whom you obligingly fay I fhall bring along with

me,

me, I shall find with you—the muses of the great simple country, not the little fine-lady mufes of Richmond-hill.

I have lived so long in the noise, or at least the distant din of the town, that I begin to forget what retirement is; with you I shall enjoy it in its highest elegance, and purest simplicity. The mind will not only be foothed into peace, but enlivened into harmony. My compliments attend all at Hagley, and particularly her * who gives it charms to you it never had before.

Believe me to be ever,

With the greateft refpect,

Moft affectionately yours,

JAMES THOMSON.

* Lucy Fortefcue, daughter of Hugh Fortefcue, Efq. of Filleigh, in the county of Devon, married

Thomson's Letter to his Sister, Mrs. Jean Thomson, at Lanark.

Hagley, in Worcestershire,
October 4th, 1747.

MY DEAR SISTER,

I THOUGHT you had known me better than to interpret my silence into a decay

to Mr. Lyttelton in the year 1742, whose amiable qualities, exemplary conduct, and uniform practice of religion and virtue, rendered her the delight and regret of all her acquaintance. She died in the beginning of the year 1746, in the 29th year of her age, leaving her husband one son, Thomas, the late Lord Lyttelton, and a daughter, Lucy, married in the year 1765 to Lord Valentia. Who has not seen and wept over the beautiful monody confecrated to her memory by the good Lord Lyttelton? If there is a living soul that has read it without emotion, I envy not their condition upon a throne.

It

decay of affection, especially as your be-
haviour has always been such as rather to
increase than to diminish it.   Don't imagine, because I am a bad correspondent,
that I can ever prove an unkind friend and
brother.   I must do myself the justice to

It is full of every thing that gives dignity to man.
Her epitaph at Hagley is less known.—

" Made to engage all hearts, and charm all eyes,
" Tho' meek, magnanimous; tho' witty, wise:
" Polite, as all her life in courts had been;
" Yet good, as she the world had never seen:
" The noble fire of an exalted mind
" With gentlest female tenderness combin'd.
" Her speech was the melodious voice of love;
" Her song, the warbling of the vernal grove;
" Her eloquence was sweeter than her song,
" Soft as her heart, and as her reason strong.
" Her form each beauty of her mind express'd;
" Her mind was virtue, by the Graces dress'd.

tell

tell you, that my affections are naturally very fixed and conftant; and if I had ever reafon of complaint againft you (of which, by the bye, I have not the leaft fhadow), I am confcious of fo many defects in myfelf, as difpofe me to be not a little charitable and forgiving.

It gives me the trueft heartfelt fatiffaction to hear you have a good kind hufband, and are in eafy contented circumftances: but were they otherwife, that would only awaken and heighten my tendernefs towards you. As our good and tender-hearted parents did not live to receive any material teftimonies of that higheft human gratitude I owed them (than which nothing could have given me more pleafure), the only return I can make them now, is by kindnefs to thofe

they

they left behind them.   Would to God
poor Lizzy* had lived longer, to be a farther witnefs of the truth of what I fay,
and that I might have had the pleafure of
feeing

* Elizabeth, married to Mr. Bell, mother of the
prefent Dr. Bell, rector of the parifh of Coldftream,
in Berwickfhire, a gentleman who poffeffes much
of the worth and genius of his uncle, and who is
now employed in preparing a new and collated
edition of Thomfon's Works, with a more correct
account of his life than has hitherto appeared; in
which pious work I have done myfelf the honour
to afford fome little affiftance in the collection of
materials.   To this edition it is propofed to prefix
an engraving from the poet's buft in Weftminfter
Abbey, and another from the fketch of a monument
drawn by Mr. Hicky, which was tranfmitted to the
Earl of Buchan by Sir Jofhua Reynolds.

The text of this new edition for the Seafons is
intended to be that in 4to. of the year 1730, in
which Autumn made its firft appearance: the addi-
tions

feeing once more a fister who so truly deferved my efteem and love.   But she is happy, while we muft toil a little longer here below: let us however do it cheerfully and gratefully, fupported by the pleafing hope of meeting yet again on a fafer fhore, where to recollect the ftorms and difficulties of life will not perhaps be inconfiftent with that blifsful ftate.   You did right to call your daughter by her name, for you muft needs have had a

tions and alterations to be printed in italics.   The following is a ftatement of the additional lines made to the Seafons after that edition :

			lines
To Spring	-	-	85
Summer	-	-	599
Autumn	-	-	96
Winter	-	-	188
			968

particular

particular tender friendſhip for one another, endeared as you were by nature, by
having paſſed the affectionate years of your
youth together, and by that great ſoftener
and engager of hearts, mutual hardſhip.
That it was in my power to eaſe it
a little, I account one of the moſt ex-
quiſite pleaſures of my life.—But enough
of this melancholy, though not unpleaſ-
ing ſtrain.

I eſteem you for your ſenſible and
diſintereſted advice to Mr. Bell, as you
will ſee by my letter to him: as I approve
entirely of his marrying again, you may
readily aſk me, why I don't marry at all?
My circumſtances have hitherto been ſo
variable and uncertain in this fluctuating
world, as induce to keep me from engaging in ſuch a ſtate; and now, though
they are more ſettled, and of late (which

you

you will be glad to hear) confiderably improved, I begin to think myfelf too far
advanced in life for fuch youthful undertakings, not to mention fome other petty
reafons that are apt to ftartle the delicacy
of difficult old bachelors. I am, however,
not a little fufpicious, that was I to pay a
vifit to Scotland (which I have fome
thoughts of doing foon), I might poffibly
be tempted to think of a thing not eafily
repaired if done amifs. *I have always
been of opinion, that none make better wives
than the ladies of Scotland;* and yet who
more forfaken than they, while the gentlemen are continually running abroad all
the world over? Some of them, it is true,
are wife enough to return for a wife.—
You fee I am beginning to make intereft
already with the Scots ladies. But no
more of this infectious fubject.—Pray let

me hear from you now and then; and though I am not a regular correspondent, yet perhaps I may mend in that respect. Remember me kindly to your husband *, and believe me to be

Your most affectionate brother,

JAMES THOMSON.

(Addressed) To Mrs. Thomson, in Lanark.

BUT

* Mr. Thomson was rector of the grammar school at Lanark, and from him, or Mrs. Thomson, Mr. Boswell obtained a copy of the original of this letter, which original is now in the possession of Mr. James Craig, architect, Thomson's youngest sister's son, who is likewise possessed of copies of Thomson's juvenile poems, of his snuff-box, and seal of arms, which hung at his watch, and of his original portrait painted by Hudson, for Mr. Millar, the bookseller, which was presented to him by Lady Grant, first married to that worthy friend of the

poet's,

BUT the higheſt encomium of Thom-
ſon is to be given him on account of his attachment to the cauſe of political and civil
liberty.   A free conſtitution of government, or what I would beg leave to call
the *autocracy* of the people, is the panacea
of moral diſeaſes, and after having been
ſought for in vain for ages, has been diſ-
covered in the boſom of truth, on the
right hand of common ſenſe, and at the
feet of philoſophy ; the printing preſs has
been the diſpenſary, and half the world

poet's, and was a daughter of Johnſon, the engraver
to the Bank of Scotland.

Lord Buchan preſented to Mr. Craig the plaſter
of Paris caſt of the buſt of Thomſon, which was
intended to have been crowned on Ednam-Hill, and
he gave a ſketch for a monument to the memory of
his uncle for that conſpicuous ſituation.

have

have become voluntary patients of this healing remedy.

It is glorious for Thomson's memory that he should have described the platform of a perfect government, as Milton described the platform of a perfect garden—the one in the midst of Gothic institutions of feudal origin, and the other in the midst of clipped yews and spouting lions.

Eighteen years after Thomson's death the late Lord Chatham agreed with me in making this remark; and when I said, " But, Sir, what will become of poor England, that doats on the imperfections of her pretended constitution?" he replied, " My dear Lord, the gout will dispose of me soon enough to prevent me from feeling the consequences of this infatuation: but before the end of this century either the parliament will reform itself from

within,

within, or be reformed with a vengeance
from without." Pythonick fpeech, fpeedily
to be verified !

" Should then the times arrive (which Heaven avert!)
" That Britons bend unnerv'd, not by the force
" Of arms, more generous, and more manly, quell'd,
" But by *corruption's* foul-dejecting arts,
" Arts impudent, and grofs ! by *their own* gold,
" *In part* beftow'd to bribe them to give *all :*
" With party raging, or immers'd in *floth*,
" Should *fhamelefs pens* for fly corruption plead;
" The hired affaffins of the commonweal !
" That nation fhall another Carthage be."

Britons ! be firm !—nor let corruption fly
Twine round your hearts indiffoluble chains !
The fteel of Brutus burft the groffer bonds
By Cæfar caft o'er Rome ; but ftill remain'd
The foft enchanting fetters of the mind,
And *other Cæfars* rofe. Determin'd hold·
Your INDEPENDANCE ; for, *that* once deftroy'd,

Unfounded,

Unfounded, FREEDOM is a morning dream,
That flits aërial from the spreading eye.

No wonder that, when the brutal Johnson tried to read liberty when it firſt appeared, he ſoon deſiſted, when Johnſon's
countrymen try to read France's liberty,
and deſiſt!

" Pudet hæc opprobria nobis, et dici potuiſſe,
" Et non potuiſſe refelli !

Though I have not the tranſcendent
honour of being a member of the Britiſh
parliament, let not the powerful deſpiſe
my ſayings—I am the voice of one cry-
ing in the wildernefs of politics—*Make
ſtraight your ways, for the empire of de-
luſion is at an end.*

*Thomſon to Mr. Paterſon, of the Leeward Iſlands *.*

DEAR PATERSON,

IN the firſt place, and previouſly to my letter, I muſt recommend to your favour and protection, Mr. James Smith, ſearcher

---

* Mr. Paterſon, a companion of Thomſon, afterwards his deputy as ſurveyor general of the Leeward Iſlands, and his ſucceſſor in the office, uſed to write out fair copies of his works, ſeveral of which are in my collection. This gentleman, as Murdoch informs us, courted the Tragic Muſe, and wrote a piece in that line, with Arminius for its hero.

When he preſented it to the manager of Drury-lane play-houſe, the hand-writing of Edward and Eleonora being immediately recogniſed, it was ſcouted, and he was glad to ſell it for a trifle to a good-natured bookſeller.

Murdoch's Life of Thomſon.

in

in St. Chriftopher's, and I beg of you, as occafion fhall ferve, and as you find he merits it, to advance him in the bufinefs of the cuftoms. He is warmly recommended to me by Sargent, who in verity turns out one of the beft men of our youthful acquaintance, honeft, honourable, friendly, and generous.—If we are not to oblige one another, life becomes a paltry felfifh affair, a pitiful morfel in a corner! Sargent is fo happily married, that I could almoft fay, the fame cafe happen to us all.

That I have not anfwered feveral letters of yours, is not owing to the want of friendfhip, and the fincereft regard for you; but you know me well enough to account for my filence, without my faying any more upon that head; befides, I have very little to fay, that is worthy to

be

be tranfmitted over the great ocean.   The world either futilifes * fo much, or we grow fo dead to it, that its tranfactions make but a feeble impreffion on us.   † Retirement and nature are more and more my paffion every day; and now, even now, the charming time comes on: heaven is juft upon the point, or rather in the very act, of giving earth a green gown.   The voice of the nightingale is heard in our lane ‡.

You

* A verb coined by Thomfon from the adjective futile.

† On this account it has been fuggefted, that the moft proper monument for Thomfon would be a modeft Doric portico, adjoining to a cottage ftored with the beft books on natural hiftory, to be kept by fome of the poet's poor relations, with a falary.

‡ The bird-catchers about London generally obferve the fong of the nightingale in the firft or

fecond

You muſt know that I have enlarged my rural domain much to the ſame dimenſions you have done yours—the two fields next to me; from the firſt of which I have walled—no, no,—paled in about as much as my garden conſiſted of before; ſo that the walk runs round the hedge, where you may figure me walking any time of the day, and ſometimes under night. For you, I imagine you reclining under cedars and palmettos, and there enjoying more magnificent ſlumbers than are known to the pale climates of the

ſecond week of April. This letter of Thomſon's having no date, it is impoſſible to determine exactly from circumſtances when it was written; but as the firing began at Maeſtricht in the firſt week, it may be gueſſed that the letter was written about the middle of the month, ſince he ſpeaks in the cloſe of the letter of the news of the ſiege being freſh.

north;

north ;. flumbers rendered awful and divine, by the folemn ftillnefs and deep fervors of the torrid noon. At other times I imagine you drinking punch in groves of lime or orange trees, gathering pine apples from hedges as commonly as we may blackberries, poetifing under lofty laurels, or making love under full-fpread myrtles.—But to lower 'my ftyle a little—as I am fuch a genuine lover of gardening, why don't you remember me in that inftance, and fend me fome feeds of things that might fucceed here during the fummer, though they cannot perfect their feeds fufficiently in this, to them, ungenial climate, to propagate ?—in the which cafe is the calliloo; that, from the feed it bore here, produced plants puny, rickctty, and good for nothing. There are other things certainly with you, not

yet

yet brought over hither, that might flourifh here in the fummer-time, and live
tolerably well, provided they were fhel-
tered during the winter in a green-houfe.

You will give me no fmall pleafure,
by fending me, from time to time, fome
of thefe feeds, if it were no more than to
amufe me in making the trial *.

* The amufements of Thomfon were chiefly the
contemplation of nature, the ftudy of natural hiftory as a fcience, voyages and travels, and the philofophy of civil hiftory; of which laft he has given
an excellent fpecimen in his Liberty, as he has of
the firft in his Seafons and Caftle of Indolence.
Gardening, except in the ftiff ornamental ftyle of
Holland, had made but little progrefs in England
in the days of Thomfon. There were no Curtifes,
Aytouns, or Forfythes, ftill lefs any Wheatlys or
Walpoles. Philip Miller, the author of the Gardener's Dictionary, was almoft the only man who
could be of ufe to Thomfon in his refearches.

With

With regard to the brother gardeners, you ought to know, that, as they are half vegetables, the animal part of them will never have ſpirit enough to conſent to the tranſplanting of the vegetable into diſtant dangerous climates: they, happily for themſelves, have no other idea but to dig on here, eat, drink, ſleep, and kiſs their wives.

As to more important buſineſs, I have nothing to write to you. You know beſt the courſe of it. Be (as you always muſt be) juſt and honeſt; but if you are un-happily romantic, you ſhall come home without money, and write a tragedy on yourſelf. Mr. Lyttelton told me that the Grenvilles and he had ſtrongly recom-mended the perſon the governor and you propoſed for that conſiderable office, lately fallen vacant in your department, and that

there

there were good hopes of succeeding. He told me also that Mr. P. had said it was not to be expected that offices such as that is, for which the greatest interest is made here at home, could be accorded to your recommendation : but that, as to the middling or inferior offices, if there was not some particular reason to the contrary, regard would be had thereto. This is all that can be reasonably desired; and if you are not infected with a certain Creolean distemper (whereof I am persuaded your soul will utterly resist the contagion, as I hope your body will that of their natural ones), there are few men so capable of that unperishable happiness, that peace and satisfaction of mind that proceed from being reasonable and moderate in our desires, as you are. These are the treasures, dug from an inexhaustible mine in our own breasts ;

which

which, like thofe in the kingdom of heaven, the ruft of time cannot corrupt, nor
thieves break through and fteal. I muft
learn to work at this mine a little more,
being ftruck off from a certain hundred
pounds a year which you know I had.
Weft, Mallet, and I were all routed in one
day. If you would know why—out of
refentment to our friend* in Argyll-ftreet.

Yet

* George, afterwards Lord Lyttelton.—Whether
we contemplate the character of this worthy man in
public or private life, we are juftified in affirming that
he abounded in virtues not only fufficient to create
reverence and efteem, but to excite the affectionate
remembrance of all who had the honour and pleafure of his acquaintance. " His wit was nature by
" the Graces dreft"——

 " His was the large ambitious wifh,
 " To make men bleft; the figh for fuffering worth
 " Loft in obfcurity; the noble fcorn

" Of

Yet I have hopes given me of having it restored with interest, some time or other. Ah! *that some time or other is a great deceiver.* Coriolanus has not yet appeared upon the stage, from the little dirty jealousy of Tullus *—I mean of him who was desired to act Tullus—towards him †

" Of tyrant pride; the fearless great resolve,
" Th' awaken'd throb for virtue and for fame,
" The sympathies of love and friendship dear ;
" With all the social offspring of the heart."

* Garrick.

† Quin.—Those who wish to amuse themselves with the broils of the theatre may consult Davies's Dramatic Miscellanies, and his Life of Garrick, for the campaigns (as the theatricals are pleased to call them) of the winters 47 and 48.—For my own part, I admire the great Frederick of Prussia, who coming to his concert, and finding the musicians quarrelling, exclaimed with a good-natured smile—" Arrangez vous, coquins."

who

who can alone act Coriolanus. Indeed, the firſt has entirely jockeyed the laſt off the ſtage for this ſeaſon; but I believe he will return on him next ſeaſon, like a giant in his wrath. Let us have a little more patience, Paterſon; nay, let us be cheerful. At laſt all will be well; at leaſt all will be over—*here* I mean: God forbid it ſhould be hereafter. But as ſure as there is a God, that will not be ſo *. Now that I am prating of myſelf, know that after fourteen or fifteen years, the Caſtle of Indolence comes abroad in a

* It is pleaſing to ſee the laſt expreſſions of the poet's confidence, that the form of the ſoul is eternal; that great ſpirits periſh not with the body. There may be worthleſs veſſels, and there may be veſſels fitted for deſtruction; but of all that Heaven has endowed with feelings to enjoy it, nothing ſhall be loſt, and the King of Heaven ſhall raiſe it up again at the laſt day!

fort-

fortnight *.   It will certainly travel as far as Barbadoes.   You have an apartment in it, as a night penfioner, which you may remember I filled up for you during our delightful party at North Ham.   Will ever thefe days return again ? Don't you remember your eating the raw fifh that was never caught ? All our friends are

* The Caftle of Indolence is the fineft poem of the kind in any language—worthy of the ripened tafte of Thomfon, and of a polifhed age.

O thou, whofe genius, powerful yet refin'd,
Whofe bard-like virtues, and confummate fkill
To touch the finer fprings that move the heart,
Join'd to whate'er the Graces could beftow,
And all Apollo's animating fire,
Gave thee with pleafing dignity to fhine
At once the friend, the ornament, and joy
Of Phœbus' fons—permit a rural mufe,
Thus in thy words to hail thy honour'd fhade !
Thus to proclaim thee to a downward age
The friend of virtue, liberty, and love.

pretty

pretty much in ftatu quo, except it be poor Mr. Lyttelton. He has had the fevereft trial an humane tender heart can have *: but the old phyfician Time will at laft clofe up his wounds, though there muft always remain an inward fmarting. Mitchel † is in the houfe for Aberdeen-fhire, and has fpoken, modeftly well: I hope he will be in fomething elfe foon. None deferves better: true friendfhip and humanity dwell in his heart. Gray is working hard at paffing his accounts. I fpoke to him about that affair. If he

* The death of his Lucy.

† Sir Andrew Mitchel of Thainftoun. Not a word of exaggeration. He was an excellent man. It is needlefs for me to attempt faying any thing about a man who was efteemed by Frederick the Great, and beloved by his acquaintance and rela-tions.

gives

gives you any trouble about it, even that of dunning, I fhall think of it ftrangely ; but I dare fay he is too friendly to do it. He values himfelf juftly upon being friendly to his old friends, and you are among the oldeft. Symmer is at laft tired of quality, and is going to take a femi-country houfe at Hammerfmith. I am forry that honeft fenfible Warrender (who is in town) feems to be ftunted in church preferment. He ought to be a tall cedar in the houfe of the Lord. If he is not fo at laft, it will add more fuel to my indignation, that burns already too intenfely, and throbs towards an eruption. Peter Murdoch is in town, tutor to Admiral Vernon's fon, and is in good hopes of another living in Suffolk, that country of tranquillity, where he will then burrow

himfelf

himſelf in a wife and be happy.   Good-
natured obliging Millar is as uſual.

Though the Doctor * increaſes in his
busineſs,

* Doctor Armſtrong.—Armſtrong was a worthy
man, a good phyſician, and perhaps one of the beſt
ſcientific didactic poets in the world, as appears
from his poem on the Art of preſerving Health.
Thomſon has deſcribed his abſent moods in the
Caſtle of Indolence, in the tenth ſtanza:

" With him was ſometimes join'd in ſilent walk,
" (Profoundly ſilent, for they never ſpoke)
" One ſhyer ſtill, who quite deteſted talk ;
" Oft ſtung by ſpleen, at once away he broke,
" To groves of pine, and broad o'erſhadowing oak :
" There, inly thrill'd, he wander'd all alone,
" And on himſelf his penſive fury woke ;
" He never utter'd word, ſave when firſt ſhone
" The glittering ſtar of eve—Thank Heaven ! the day
    is done."

When the good Doctor was with the Britiſh army
in

bufinefs, he does not decreafe in fpleen ;
but there is a certain kind of fpleen, that
is both humane and agreeable, like Jacques
in the play.   I fometimes have a touch of
it.—But I muft break off this chat with
you about our friends, which, were I to
indulge it, would be endlefs—As for politics—we are I believe upon the brink of
a peace.   The French at prefent are va-
pouring in the fiege of Maeftricht, at the
fame time they are mortally fick in their
marine, and through all the vitals of
France.   It is a pity we cannot continue
the war a little longer, and put their ago-
nifing trade quite to death.   This fiege,

in Flanders, as furgeon or phyfician, he was taken
prifoner one day, taking what he called a ftroll beyond the lines.   I cannot but remember with high
pleafure that worthy character.   He died September
30, 1779, much regretted by all who had the pleafure of his acquaintance.

T

I take

I take it, they mean as their laſt flouriſh in the war.—May your health, which never failed you yet, ſtill continue, till you have ſcraped together enough to return home, and live in ſome ſnug corner, as happy as the Corycius Senex, in Virgil's fourth Georgic, whom I recommend both to you and myſelf as a perfect model of the trueſt happy life. Believe me to be ever moſt ſincerely, and affectionately,

Yours, &c.

JAMES THOMSON.

ODE

ODE ON THE DEATH OF THOMSON.

BY MR. COLLINS.

The Scene on the Thames near Richmond.

I.

IN yonder grave a Druid lies,
  Where flowly winds the ftealing wave;
The year's beft fweets fhall duteous rife
  To deck its poet's fylvan grave.

II.

In yon deep bed of whifp'ring reeds
  His airy harp;* fhall now be laid,
That he, whofe heart in forrow bleeds,
  May love thro' life the foothing fhade.

III.

Then maids and youths fhall linger here,
  And while its founds at diftance fwell,
Shall fadly feem in pity's ear
  To hear the woodland pilgrim's knell.

---

* The Æolian harp.

T 2   IV. Re-

IV.

Remembrance oft shall haunt the shore
　　When Thames in summer wreaths is dreft,
And oft sufpend the dashing oar,
　　To bid his gentle spirit reft !

V.

And oft, as eafe and health retire
　　To breezy lawn, or foreft deep,
The friend shall view yon whitening * spire,
　　And 'mid the varied landfcape weep.

VI.

But thou, who own'ft that earthy bed,
　　Ah ! what will every dirge avail ;
Or tears, which love and pity shed,
　　That mourn beneath the gliding fail !

VII.

Yet lives there one, whofe heedlefs eye
　　Shall fcorn thy pale shrine glimm'ring near ?

---

* Richmond church, where Thomfon lies buried in the north-weft corner of it, below the chriftening pew, without a tablet or memorial to fay—Here Thomfon lies.

With

With him, sweet bard, may fancy die,
　　And joy desert the blooming year.

VIII.

But thou, lorn stream, whose sullen tide
　　No sedge-crown'd sisters now attend,
Now waft me from the green hill's side,
　　Whose cold turf hides the buried friend!

IX.

And see, the fairy valleys fade,
　　Dun night has veil'd the solemn view:
Yet once again, dear parted shade,
　　Meek nature's child, again adieu!

X.

The genial meads assign'd to bless
　　Thy life, shall mourn thy early doom;
Their hinds and shepherd-girls shall dress
　　With simple hands thy rural tomb.

XI.

Long, long, thy stone and pointed clay
　　Shall melt the musing Briton's eyes:
O! vales, and wild woods, shall he say,
　　In yonder grave your Druid lies.

T 3

THE

THE REVEREND MR. WILLIAM THOMSON's

(*Sometime of Queen's College, Oxford*)

ADDRESS TO THE SHADE OF THOMSON*.

HAIL, nature's poet! whom fhe taught alone
To fing her works in numbers like her own:
Sweet as the thrufh that warbles in the dale,
And foft as Philomela's tender tale.
She lent her pencil too, of wondrous pow'r,
To catch the rainbow, and to paint the flow'r
Of many mingling hues; then fmiling faid
(But firft with laurel crown'd her fav'rite's head),
" Thefe beauteous children, tho' fo fair they fhine,
" Fade in *my* feafons—let them live in *thine* ?"
And live they fhall, the charm of ev'ry eye,
Till nature fickens, and the feafons die.

---

* Thefe beautiful and applicable lines were pronounced by Lord Buchan, on Ednam Hill, on the 22d of September 1791, when he crowned the firft edition of the Seafons with a wreath of bays.

7.   *Anniverfary*

Anniverſary of Thomſon's Birth-day, 1790.

THE Earl of Buchan, deſirous of promoting a ſubſcription for erecting a monument to the memory of Thomſon on Ednam Hill, circulated letters to a conſiderable number of gentlemen of Berwick and Roxburghſhires, in the beginning of September, inviting them to celebrate the 22d of September at a Mrs. Spinks's, in Ednam village, where Sir James Pringle, Sir Alexander Don, Dr. Bell, of Coldſtream, the poet's ſiſter's ſon, and a dozen more gentlemen accordingly met, and paſſed the evening with attick feſtivity and good humour, the Earl of Buchan ſitting as præſes in the chair whereon the poet ſat when he compoſed his Caſtle of Indolence. This chair became the property of Dr. Arm-

T 4   ſtrong,

ftrong, who had it from Sir Andrew Mitchel, who left it to Mr. Elliot, and by him it was obligingly fent to accommodate the prefident member of this fociety, upon this occafion.

The gentlemen who affembled on this day refolved to meet annually on its anniverfary*, and to open a fubfcription for erecting

---

* It is remarkable that Mrs. Mary Thomfon, fifter of the poet, and mother of Mr. Craig, architect, was buried on this day; and that while Lord Buchan was on Ednam Hill to celebrate the anniverfary, the fon was dropping the laft cord into the grave of Thomfon's fifter.

The fame day likewife, though without previous concert, the fociety, at Ednam, called the Knights of the Cape, met in their hall at Ednam, to celebrate the birth-day of the bard. Mr. Woods, the comedian, recited a handfome occafional poem of his own compofition in honour of the day. On the toaft

being

erecting a monument on Ednam Hill, requesting the Earl of Buchan to apply to the curators of Mr. Cuthbert, of Ednam, the proprietor of Ednam, a minor, for a grant of the spot neceffary for the building and its appurtenances.

In returning from this meeting the Earl of Buchan's carriage, in which he was

being given to the memory of Thomfon, Mr. Woods recited, from a poem of Dr. Langhorne's, the conteft of the Seafons, who are reprefented as appealing to Thomfon to decide on their refpective merits.   At proper intervals he afterwards delivered paffages from the four Seafons of the author, each being followed by fongs applicable to the refpective fubjects, by other members of the fociety.   Mr. Woods then recited a number of paffages, felected by him from Thomfon's Poem of Liberty; after which Rule Britannia was fung by the whole company on their legs, with which this attick entertainment concluded.

accom-

accompanied by Sir Alexander Don, and Mr. Thomas Potts, writer at Kelſo, was overturned by a reſtive horſe on the approach to Ednam Bridge, but without any worſe conſequences than the breaking of the machine. In the ſucceeding year, Lord Buchan obtained a conceſſion of promiſe from the curators of Mr. Cuthbert, for a grant of the ſpot neceſſary for erecting a monument on the ſummit-of Ednam Hill, and he circulated letters to the gentlemen who had attended the former anniverſary, and to many other perſons of diſtinction and learning in Scotland ; to Meſſrs. Hayley, Maſon, Beattie, and Burns. But very few gentlemen paid any attention to the notification ; a caſt from the buſt of the poet in Weſtminſter Abbey, which had been generouſly tranſmitted by Mr. Coutts, banker at London, to be

crowned

crowned with a wreath of bays, was broken in a midnight frolick during the race week on the 16th of September; and the Earl of Buchan contented himfelf with impofing a wreath of laurel, dreffed by Mr. Robert Craig, architect, the poet's fifter's fon, on a copy of the Seafons, printed 1730, in 4to, being the firft complete edition prefented by the poet to his father, addreffing the fhade of the poet, in the beautiful apoftrophe compofed for a blank leaf of the Seafons by the Rev. Mr. William Thomfon, of Queen's College, Oxon, a copy of which is here publifhed.   I fhall now fubmit to the perufal of the reader, Mr. Burns * the Airfhire

bard's

---

* Robert Burns, of Airfhire, a farmer's fon, remarkable for a genuine vein of Doric poetry, and for his fuperior abilities and good fenfe, which have ena-

bled

bard's apology for not attending the meeting, and his addrefs to the fhade of Thomfon.

MY LORD,

LANGUAGE finks under the ardour of my feelings, when I would thank your Lordfhip for the honour, the very great honour, you have done me, in inviting me to the coronation of the buft of Thomfon.

bled him to efcape the fhipwreck of the fons of Apollo, by continuing his profeffion of a farmer.

Mr. Millar, of Dalfwinton, a gentleman well known by his great genius in mechanics, and his eminence as a banker, generoufly gave the young poet a comfortable and agreeable farm at Ellifland, near Dumfries, where he wooes his ruftic mufe in eafe with that native dignity which muft ever arife from fuperior tafte. " Spernit humum fugiente " penna."

—In

—In my firſt enthuſiaſm, on reading the card you did me the honour to write to me, I overlooked every obſtacle, and determined to go; but I fear it will not be in my power.—A week or two in the very middle of my harveſt, is what I much doubt I dare not venture on.—I once already made a pilgrimage *up* the whole courſe of the Tweed, and fondly would I take the ſame delightful journey *down* the windings of that charming ſtream.

Your Lordſhip hints at an ode for the occaſion: but who would write after Collins? I read over his verſes to the memory of Thomſon, and deſpaired. I attempted three or four ſtanzas in the way of addreſs to the ſhade of the bard, on crowning his buſt.—I trouble your Lordſhip with the incloſed copy of them, which

I am

I am afraid will be but too convincing a
proof how unequal I am to the talk you
would obligingly affign me.—However,
it affords me an opportunity of approaching your Lordfhip, and declaring how
fincerely I have the honour to be,

    My Lord,

      Your Lordfhip's highly obliged,

       And moft devoted humble fervant,

          ROBERT BURNS.

Ellifland, near Dumfries,
  29th Auguft, 1791.

ADDRESS TO THE SHADE OF THOMSON,

On crowning his Buſt with a Wreath of Bays.

I.

WHILE virgin Spring, by Eden's flood,
  Unfolds her tender mantle green;
Or pranks the ſod in frolic mood,
  Or tunes Eolian ſtrains between;

II.

While Summer with a matron grace
  Retreats to Dryburgh's cooling ſhade,
Yet oft delighted ſtops to trace
  The progreſs of the ſpiky blade;

III.

While Autumn, benefactor kind,
  By Tweed erects her aged head,
And ſees, with ſelf-approving mind,
  Each creature on her bounty fed;

IV.

While maniac Winter rages o'er
  The hills whence claſſic Yarrow flows,

Rouſing

Roufing the turbid torrent's roar,
  Or sweeping wild a wafte of fnows;

V.

So long, fweet poet of the year,
  Shall bloom that wreath thou well haft won,
While Scotia with exulting tear
  Proclaims that Thomfon was her fon.

THE

THE EARL OF BUCHAN'S INVITATION TO SIR JOHN
SINCLAIR, OF ULBSTER, TO BE PRESENT
AT THE FESTIVAL OF THOMSON.   1791.

SINCLAIR! thou phœnix of the frozen Thule!
O shape thy course to Tweda's lovely stream,
Whose lucid, sparkling, gently flowing course
Winds like Ilissus through a land of song:
Not as of old, when, like the Theban twins,
Her rival children tore each other's breasts,
And stained her silver wave with kindred blood:
But proudly glittering through a happy land,
The yellow harvests bend along her fields;
The golden orchards glow with blushing fruits;
Green are her pastoral banks, white are her flocks,
That safely stray where barb'rous Edward raged;
And where the din of clashing arms was heard
We hear the carols of the happy swains,
Free as their lords, and with the purring looms,
Hark, hark, the weaver's merry roundelay!
The charming song of Scotland's better day:
'Tis liberty, sweet liberty alone
Can give a lustre to the northern sun.
" Come when the Virgin gives the beauteous days,
            U   " And

" And Libra weighs in equal fcales the year;"

Come, and to Thomfon's gentle fhade repair,

And pour libations to his virtuous mufe,

Where firft he drew the flame of vital air,

" Where firft his feet did prefs the virgin fnow,

" And where he tuned his charming Doric reed."

Perhaps where Thomfon fired the foul of fong,

Some voice may whifper in Æolian ftrains

To him who, wand'ring near his parent ftream,

Shall o'er the placid blue profound of air

Receive the genius of his paffing fhade.

Come then, my Sinclair, leave empiric Pitt,

And raging Burke, and all the hodge-podge fry

Of Tory Whigs, and whiggifh Tory knaves,

And bathe thy genius in thy coantry's fame :

Let Burke write pamphlets, and let Pitt declaim ;

Let us feek honour in our country's weal.

Eulogy

Eulogy of Thomson, the Poet, delivered by the Earl of Buchan, on Ednam Hill, when he crowned the first edition of the Seasons with a wreath of bays, on the 22d of September, 1791.

Gentlemen,

IT has been the custom of that great and truly to be respected nation of the French, to pronounce, at the meetings of men of genius, learning, and taste, the praises of the illustrious dead; and this custom has been adopted by other countries, as, emerging from barbarity, they became gradually sensible of the infinite superiority of men imbued with science, learning, and taste, over the ignorant creatures of imperial power.

U 2

They

They faw, and deplored, the rude inſtitutions of their ſavage anceſtors on the
page of hiſtory, inſtitutions which covered
men with honours, and beſtrung them
with ribbands, according to the guſt and
prejudice of illiterate princes, and left the
real benefactors and ornaments of ſociety
to languiſh or to paſs unnoticed in ob-
ſcurity,   Fortunately born as we have
been in the age of a Frederick the Great,
and of a Waſhington, all men poſſeſſed
of any taſte or feeling (and may I add)
of common ſenſe, have rejoiced, and do
now rejoice, to behold the dignity of human nature beginning to appear amidſt
the ruins of Gothic ſuperſtition and
tyranny, and the immortal Pruſſia, ſtanding like a herald in the proceſſion of ages,
to mark the beginning of that order of
                                        men

men who are to banish from the earth the silly delusions of worthless priest-craft, and the monstrous prerogatives of despotic authority.

I think myself happy to have this day the task assigned to me of endeavouring to do justice to the memory of Thomson, which has been prophanely touched by the rude hands of the pedantic Samuel Johnson, whose fame and reputation indicates the decline of taste in a country that, after having produced an Alfred, a Wallace, a Bacon, a Napier, a Newton, a Buchanan, a Milton, a Hampden, a Fletcher, and a Thomson, can submit to be bullied under the rod of a school-master, or to be led by the strings of the satchel of a petulant school-boy!

Scotland, Gentlemen, though now full

of

of men who are above servile compliance with the power of the day, was, in the days of Thomson, a nation of proud and poor nobles and difpirited vaffals. Except Belhaven and Fletcher, whom he hardly faw, and Argyll, Stair, Marchmont, and other free fpirits, whom delicacy forbids me to mention, there were few in the kingdom who could encourage the poet to rife above the mediocrity of a fettered ftudent of divinity, or to imbue his mind with that noble fentiment of independence by which his life and his writings are characterifed and diftinguifhed. In the family of Jervifwood, to which he was introduced by the kindred of his mother, he received the earlieft attentions; and fome verfes of his addreffed to one of that family, for the ufe of fome books,

. are,

are, I believe, still preserved as a specimen of his infantine genius.

That the lady indiscreetly alluded to in the Life of Thomson, should have encouraged him to try his fortune in London, is highly probable; but that she should have deserted him afterwards agrees not with the nature of a spontaneous patronage; for nothing is more natural to patrons than the desire of seeing due attention paid to their recommendations, and following out the objects of their protection to the attainment of honour, that shall reflect upon themselves.

The trifling story about his losing his bundle on his way from Wapping to Mallet's house in London, and the want of his shoes, is in the odour of that vulgar malevolence, which gives a *race* to the works of the *savage* biographer.

U 4

The

The only occasion, when I had the mischance to meet Johnson, was at old Strahan's (the translator of the six first books of the Æneid), in Suffolk Street, where I found him and Mallet cobling these books for publication; and there I remember to have heard them repeating this story with glee, after having cut down Dryden, Gawin, Douglas, Trapp, and the other predecessors of poor Strahan, in the translation of the Æneid.

Such are the annals of critics, and poetasters, and with this blacking let them be handed down to posterity, with the shoes of the bard of Ednam.

We are much indebted to Aaron Hill for his kindness to Thomson, and his handsome lines in compliment to Scotland, now in every mouth: no more poetry and prophecy, but matter of fact!

How

How different an Aaron Hill, a Thomas Pennant, and a Thomas Newte, from a Samuel Johnson!

Why, says Johnson, are the dedications to Winter, and the other Seasons, contrary to custom, left out in Thomson's collected works? I will tell you, shade of Johnson. *Because little men* disappear when great men take their proper station.

The Countess of Hertford, says Johnson, used to invite every summer some poet to hear her verses; and Thomson, who was called for that purpose, took more delight in carousing with Lord Hertford and his friends, than in assisting her Ladyship's poetical operations, who therefore never gave the poet another summons.

That no earl or countess ever gave

Johnson

Johnson an invitation to the country can excite no wonder, nor that Thomson's genius and independant spirit should lead him to prefer wit and the social board of an accomplished family, to the manufacture of courtly verses, for a verse-sick countess.

Lord Chatham, Lord Temple, Lord Lyttelton, Sir Andrew Mitchel, Dr. Armstrong, Mr. Gray, of Richmond-Hill, and the oily man of God, I have often had the pleasure to hear on the subject of Thomson. All of them agreed in the testimony of his being a gentleman at all points, and a gentleman by God, as well as a poet by nature, far above the degree of our modern poets, that are infused into the house of bards, in imitation of our modern system of peerage.

Of

Of Johnfon's criticifm on the Poem of Thomfon, entitled Liberty, I fhall fay nothing; but I will take the liberty to fay that Britain knows nothing of the liberty that Thomfon celebrates!

Thomfon

Thomson to the Sister of his Amanda, at
Bath.

Kew Lane, Nov. 27, 1742.

MADAM,

GIVE me leave to say that, among all your friends, nobody longs more ardently after the full establishment of your health than I do: first, and foremost, upon your own personal account; and secondly, from more selfish motives, that you may soon return to supply to us the want of the sun by your company. You may, perhaps, think this compliment a little high-strained; whereas, upon the faith of a melancholy man, and as I hope to laugh again, I would, for three or four hours of your company, give three or four months of such days as these. But at the

                                                  same

fame time I muft be fo bold as to add, that though it be downright deep November, and you, Mifs Berry, and Mifs Young abfent, none of us will pufh the compliment fo far as to verify the French author's obfervation, who begins his book thus—It was in the month of November, when Englifhmen hang and drown themfelves—And yet, I am difmal enough, fometimes, nay—would you believe it?— as it were, vapoured. Do, dear Mrs. Robertfon, make hafte to be well.

Sorely do I grieve not to have been one of your 'fquires that day you fet out; for, befides the ferious pleafure of attending you and your companions, I hear very diverting accounts of the journey, particularly of David's navigation on horfeback; how it blew a hard gale of riding with him, driving him now a great

way

way on one side, then, helm-a-lee, on
the other; how he had almoſt committed
piracy on the highway; and how he was
next morning, while aſleep, deſerted by
the ſhip's crew, and left among the ſa-
vages.   I am furthermore informed that,
being thereunto moved by the inſtigation
of a galled backſide, and not having the
fear of the ladies before his eyes, he was
guilty of high treaſon againſt their ſovereign beauty, by uttering certain baſe,
ſcandalous, and traiterous words, for the
which he muſt in due time undergo his
trial; George Scot *, judge; James Robertſon †, attorney general; and William

* George Lewis Scot, afterwards ſub-preceptor
to the king, and one of the commiſſioners of ex-
ciſe.

† Mr. Robertſon, ſurgeon to the houſehold at
Kew.

Paterſon

Paterſon *, foreman of the jury. But, by their mutual accuſations, I find there is a heavy charge againſt them all.

To think of leaving, nay, for ſome time actually to have left, diſtreſſed ladies under their protection, to travel in the dark through infamous places, through Maidenhead Thicket, where · ſo many robberies had been committed the very day before, is ſuch a ſtain upon all chivalry, as their return cannot entirely wipe off. They were, indeed, upon the brink of perdition; for had they not returned, their ſwords muſt have been broken over their heads, their arms reverſed, and the ban of all gallantry publiſhed againſt them. Nobody would have drunk, no-

* Paterſon, formerly mentioned, who was then a clerk in a compting houſe, afterwards Thomſon's deputy as ſurveyor of the Leeward Iſlands.

body

body would have toafted with them, and nothing but making two or three campaigns in the fervice of that heroic lady, the Queen of Hungary, could have reftored them to any degree of honour.

I hope the ladies have at laft got their clothes. To be at Bath, yet debarred from the rooms, muft have been a cruel fituation to fuch as knew lefs how to converfe with, and enjoy themfelves— the very fituation of Tantalus! up to the lip in diverfions, without being able to catch a drop of them.—And yet, notwithftanding all thefe diverfions, I do, from my foul, moft fincerely pity you, to be fo long doomed to a place fo delightfully tirefome. Delightfully, did I fay? No; it is merely a fcene of waking dreams, where nothing but the phantoms of pleafure fly about, without any fub-

ftance

ftance or reality.   What a round of filly amufements, what a giddy circle of *no-thing* do thefe children of a larger fize run every day! Nor does it only give a gay vertigo to the head, it has equally a bad influence on the heart.   When the head is full of nothing but drefs, and fcandal, and dice, and cards, and rowly powly, can the heart be fenfible to thofe fine emotions, thofe tender, humane, generous paffions that form the foul of all virtue and happinefs! Ah! then, ye lovers, never think to make any impreffion on the hearts of the diffipated fair.   So could I proceed in my tedious homily; but I afk pardon for railing at a place you are obliged to be at, and which I hope will reftore you to perfect health.   Yes, that reconciles me to it again; and if my letter was not already too long, I would make its panegyric.

X   May

May I flatter myfelf with the hopes of hearing from you? If you fend me but your three names, and above them—" We are well," I fhall be glad even of that.— Madam, I am forry to acquaint you, that your hufband, once famous for hofpitality, has loft it all fince you left this place. Pray be fo good as to lay your commands upon him, to treat us fome night or other with a bowl of punch, that we may drink your healths. My beft compliments, my moft hearty refpects, my—in fhort, all the good wifhes my heart can form, attend you all! Believe me to be,

With the utmoft refpect,

Madam,

Your, and Mifs Young's,

And Mifs Berry's,

Devoted humble fervant,

JAMES THOMSON.

Humorous

Humorous Epiſtle to a Friend, on his Travels.

December 7, 1742.

TRUSTY AND WELL-BELOVED DOG,

HEARING you are gone abroad to ſee the world, as they call it, I cannot forbear, upon this occaſion, tranſmitting you a few thoughts.

It may ſeem preſumption in me to pretend to give you any inſtruction; but you muſt know, that I am a dog of conſiderable experience. Indeed I have not improved ſo much as I might have done, by my juſtly deſerved misfortunes: the caſe very often of my betters.

However, a little I have learned; and ſometimes, while I ſeemed to lie aſleep before the fire, I have overheard the converſation óf your travellers.

In

In the firſt place, I will not ſuppoſe that you are gone abroad an illiterate cub, juſt eſcaped from the laſh of your keeper, and running wild about the world like a dog who has loſt his maſter, utterly unacquainted with the proper knowledge, manners, and converſation of dogs.

Theſe are the public jeſts of every country through which they run poſt, and frequently they are avoided as if they were mad dogs. None will converſe with them but thoſe who ſhear, ſometimes even ſkin them, and often they return home like a dog who has loſt his tail. In ſhort, theſe travelling puppies do nothing elſe but run after foreign bitches, learn to dance, cut capers, play tricks, and admire your fine outlandiſh howling: though in my opinion, our vigorous, deep-mouthed Britiſh note is better muſic.

If

If a timely stop is not put to this, the genuine breed of our ancient sturdy dogs will, by degrees, dwindle and degenerate into dull Dutch maftiffs, effeminate Italian lapdogs, or tawdry, impertinent French harlequins. All our once noble-throated guardians of the houfe and fold will be fucceeded by a mean courtly race, that fnarl at honeft men, flatter rogues, proudly wear badges of flavery, ribbands, collars, &c. and fetch and carry fticks at the lion's court. By the bye, my dear Marquis, this fetching and carrying of fticks is a diverfion you are too much addicted to, and, though a diverfion, unbecoming a true independent country dog. There is another dog-vice, that greatly prevails among the hungry whelps at court; but your gut is too well ftuffed to fall into that. What I mean is, patting, pawing, folicit-

X 3

ing,

ing, teafing, fnapping the morfel out of one another's mouths, being bitterly en-vious, and infatiably ravenous, nay, fome-times filching when they fafely may. Of this vice I have an inftance continually before my eyes, in that wretched animal Scrub, whofe genius is quite mifplaced here in the country. He has, befides, fuch an admirable talent at fcratching at a door, as might well recommend him to the office of a court-waiter—A word in your ear—I wifh a certain two-legged friend of mine had a little of his affiduity, Thefe canine courtiers are alfo extremely given to bark at merit and virtue, if ill-clad and poor: they have likewife a nice difcernment, with regard to thofe whom their mafter diftinguifhes: to fuch you fhall fee them go up immediately, and fawning in the moft abject manner—

baifer

baiſer leur cul. For me, it is always a maxim with me,

> To honour humble worth, and, ſcorning ſtate,
> Piſs on the proud inhoſpitable gate.

For which reaſon I go ſcattering my water every where about Richmond. And now that I am upon this topic, I muſt cite you two lines of a letter from Bounce (of celebrated memory), to Fop, a dog in the country to a dog at court. She is giving an account of her generous offspring, among which ſhe mentions two, far above the vice I now cenſure;

> One uſhers friends to Bathurſt's door,
> One fawns at Oxford's on the poor!

Charming dogs! I have little more to ſay; but only, conſidering the great mart of ſcandal you are at, to warn you againſt flattering thoſe you converſe with, and,

X 4

the

the moment they turn to go away, back-
biting them—a vice with which the dogs
of old ladies are much infected; and you
muft have been moft furioufly affected
with it here at Richmond, had you not
happened into a good family; therefore
I might have fpared this caution.—One
thing I had almoft forgot. You have a
bafe cuftom, when you chance upon a
certain fragrant exuvium, of perfuming
your carcafe with it. Fye! fye! leave
that nafty cuftom to your little, foppifh,
crop-eared dogs, who do it to conceal
their own ftink.

My letter, I fear, grows tedious. I will
detain you from your flumbers no longer,
but conclude by wifhing that the waters
and exercife may bring down your fat
fides, and that you may return a genteel
accomplifhed dog. Pray lick for me, you

happy

happy dog you, the hands of the fair ladies you have the honour to attend. I remember to have had that happiness once, when one, who fhall be namelefs, looked with an envious eye upon me.

Farewell, my dear Marquis. Return, I beg it of you, foon to Richmond; when I will treat you with fome choice fragments, a marrow-bone which I will crack for you myfelf, and a deffert of hightoafted cheefe. I am, without farther ceremony, yours fincerely,

B U F F.

Mi Dewti too Marki. X Scrub's mark.

Letter to Mrs. R. the Sifter of Amanda.

Chriftmas Day, 1742.

Madam,

I BELIEVE I am in love with fome one or all of you; for though you will not

favour

3

favour me with the fcrap of a pen, yet I cannot forbear writing to you again. Is it not however barbarous, not to fend me a few foft characters, one pretty name to cheer my eyes withal? How eafily fome people might make others happy if they would! But it is no fmall comfort to me, fince you will not write, that I fhall foon have the pleafure of being in your company. And then, though I were downright picqued, I fhall forget it all in a moment.

I cannot help telling you of a very pleafing fcene I lately faw.————In the middle of a green field there ftands a peace-ful lowly habitation; into which having entered, I beheld innocence, fweet inno-cence, afleep. Your heart would have yearned, your eyes perhaps overflowed with tears of joy, to fee how charming

he

he looked; like a young cherub dropped from Heaven, if they be so happy as to have young cherubs there.

When awaked, it is not to be imagined with what complacency and ease, what soft serenity altogether unmixed with the leaft cloud, he opened his eyes. Dancing with joy in his nurfe's arms, his eyes not only fmiled, but laughed— which put me in mind of a certain near relation of his, whom I need not name.

What delights thee fo, thou lovely babe? art thou thinking of thy mother's re-covery? does fome kind power imprefs upon thee a prefage of thy future happi-nefs under her tender care?—I took the liberty to touch him with unhallowed lips, which reftored me to the good opinion of the nurfe, who had neither forgot nor forgiven my having flighted that favour

5once.

once. While thus I gazed with sincere
and virtuous satisfaction, I could most
pathetically have addressed the gay
wretches of the age, the joyless inmates
of Bachelor's Hall *, and was ready to
repeat Milton's divine Hymn on Mar-
riage:

> Hail, wedded Love! mysterious law, true source
> Of human offspring, sole propriety
> In Paradise of all things common else!
> By thee adulterous lust was driven from men
> Among the bestial herds to range.; by thee,
> Founded in reason, loyal, just and pure,
> Relations dear, and all the charities
> Of father, son, and brother, first were known.
> Far be it, &c.

Now that I have been transcribing

* Bachelor's Hall, a house on Richmond Hill; so
called, from being occupied during the summer sea-
son by a society of gentlemen from London.

some

fome lines of poetry, I think I once engaged myfelf while walking in Kew-lane
to write two or three fongs. The following is one of them, which I have ftolen
from the Song of Solomon; from that
beautiful expreffion of Love, " Turn
away thine eyes from me, for they have
overcome me."

I.

O THOU, whofe tender ferious eyes
Expreffive fpeak the mind I love;
The gentle azure of the fkies,
The penfive fhadows of the grove:

II.

O mix their beauteous beams with mine,
And let us interchange our hearts;
Let all their fweetnefs on me fhine,
Pour'd thro' my foul be all their darts.

III.

Ah! 'tis too much! I cannot bear
At once fo foft, fo keen, a ray:

In

In pity, then, my lovely fair,
O turn thefe killing eyes away!

IV.

But what avails it to conceal
One charm, where nought but charms we fee?
'Their luftre then again reveal,
And let me, Myra, die of thee.

My beft refpects attend Mifs Young and Mifs Berry, who I hope are heartily tired of Bath, and will leave it without the leaft regret, whomfoever they leave pining behind them. I wifh you all a much happier and merrier Chriftmas than we can have without you. But in amends you will bring us along with you a gay and happy new year. Believe me to be, with the greateft refpect, and the heartieft good wifhes that all health and happinefs may ever attend you,

Madam,

Your moft obedient,

Humble fervant,

JAMES THOMSON.

VERSES ADDRESSED TO MISS YOUNG.

AH urge too late! from beauty's bondage free,
Why did I truft my liberty with thee?
And thou, why didft thou, with inhuman art,
If not refolv'd to take, feduce my heart?
Yes, yes, you faid (for lovers eyes fpeak true);
You muft have feen how faft my paffion grew:
And when your glances chanc'd on me to fhine,
How my fond foul ecftatic fprung to thine!
    But mark me, fair-one, what I now declare
Thy deep attention claims, and ferious care:
It is no common paffion fires my breaft,
I muft be wretched, or I muft be bleft!
My woes all other remedy deny;
Or, pitying, give me hope, or bid me die!

To Miss Young*, with a present of his Seasons.

ACCEPT, loved nymph! this tribute due
To tender friendſhip, love, and you ;
But with it take what breath'd the whole,
O! take to thine the poet's ſoul.
If fancy here her pow'r diſplays,
And if a heart exalts theſe lays—
You faireſt in that fancy ſhine,
And all that heart is fondly thine.

---

* Some ſlight variations have been found in different copies which have been handed about in MS. This is from the original.

THE END.